THE CRC

To: Martha
My sister in the Lord

[signature]

ii

THE CROWNS OF MEN

BY

TRACEY D. HULL

Love Walk Publications

www.lovewalkpublishing.com

Published by
Love Walk Publishing
P.O. Box 1705
Warren, MI   48090

ISBN 978-0-9838389-0-6

Printed in the United States of America

DEDICATION

This book is dedicated to my mom, my sister, and my best friend: Gustavia Hull, Beverly Hall, and Latanya Mitchell. They dwell with God now.

ACKNOWLEDGEMENTS

I would like to acknowledge my sons Guadale, Aaron, Andrew, Joe, and Sharell. You guys have been an inspiration to me. You have been very supporting and encouraging. I love you all very much.

KEY RULES OF A GOOD LIFE

- *WALK IN LOVE*

- *HAVE FAITH IN GOD*

- *LIVE ACCORDING TO GOD'S WORD*

A MAN

Don't run to this world, son, to quench your thirst.

Trust me, your Father; trust my love.

Trust me to watch and see that you come out first.

Son, I love you.

Please listen, hear, and understand.

I am your Father.

I have created you to be a leader of men.

I see your heart; I have collected your tears.

Just forget about this world and all of its fears.

I am your Father.

Don't you understand?

When trouble comes, son, just give me your hand.

So that I may show you, my Master Plan.

Son, this why I created you first: To be a man.

— T.H.

INTRODUCTION

This book is all about love the way it was intended to be. In some parts, it comes in different ways; but it comes. Love seems strange. It seems like it comes when you don't expect it, and sometimes it just happens. I think the best love comes when you let it find you.

It is my wish that this book bring healing to those many people who have given up on finding love. Most people are looking for someone to love, but they don't realize that they have to be able and willing to give love back. I was guilty of that very thing.

There are things is this book that will touch peoples' hearts — and that is my prayer. The majority of this book was spirit-inspired. I have both laughed and cried in the midst of writing it. It has helped me learn to love again.

Writing this book has made me realize that true love is the purest thing on this earth. Every man, women, and child, and even animals, want to be loved.

TABLE OF CONTENTS

CHAPTER ONE
THE CROWNS OF MEN

This story begins with Sheila, a young lady who has dedicated her life to the Lord, and prayed every day that God would send her man of God to be her husband. Sheila would pray and pray faithfully, day after day, constantly asking God to send that man, and believing that He would send him to her.

One day, when Sheila arrived at work and walked into the lobby, she heard a loud noise that sounded like a sharp thunderclap. Startled, she looked around, and was surprised to see everyone else acting as though they hadn't heard it.

Later that day, she was in a board meeting with all of the executives. Present were several men and a few women. The meeting was being held in an auditorium. Sheila was sitting in the back, and she could only see the backs of everyone else's heads.

Just before the meeting began, Sheila heard the same thunderclap noise she had heard in the lobby. At the same time, she was startled when *things* suddenly appeared on all of the men's heads. Hanging in mid-air, the things were doing all kinds of gyrations. Most of them were spinning rapidly. Suddenly the things vanished. Alarmed, she looked around quickly, wondering what the heck was going on. As with the thunderclap noise, everyone acted as though they hadn't seen or heard anything.

Later, after leaving work for the day, she went to the local mall to try and take her mind off the strange events that had happened at work.

As Sheila walked through the mall, her attention was inexplicably drawn to a group of men standing by themselves. For some reason that she couldn't figure out, they were very noticeable to her. As she walked by them, the very same thunderclap from earlier in the day echoed throughout the mall. Looking back at the men as she passed them, she saw the same *things* over the men's heads as she had seen during the board meeting. Shaking her head and rubbing her eyes, she took another look, and saw that the things were gone.

As she had done at work, Sheila looked around to see if anyone else had heard the thunderclap or seen the things; but everyone in the mall was acting normally, as though nothing unusual had occurred. Alarmed and puzzled, she said to herself, "I must be tripping out! I'd better get home!"

As soon as she walked into her apartment, Sheila called her friend, Saved Sister. When it came to matters of

God, Saved Sister didn't play around. She was a devout Bible-toting, tongue-talking, Holy-Ghost-walking sister. Whenever Sheila needed someone to pray for her, she called Saved Sister.

Sheila told Saved Sister, Some strange things are happening and the two women prayed about it. Saved Sister then said, "Girl, you need to get out more. You never get out and mingle. I tell you what. I'm going to stop over there when I get off work."

"Thanks," Sheila said, relieved that she would have the chance to talk face-to-face with Saved Sister.

When she arrived at Sheila's apartment later, Saved Sister told Sheila about a church singles meeting that was coming up, and asked her if she would like to go. Sheila responded that she'd think about it.

Saved Sister then asked, "So, do you have any thoughts as to what might be the cause of the noises you heard and the things you saw?"

Sheila took a deep breath, then began. "Girl, I believe that God is trying to tell me something. Last night I prayed all night in the spirit. The anointing was so strong that I felt God was right here in the room with me. This morning, I woke up and started praying in the spirit some more. Once I finished, it seemed like my feet were not even touching the ground. I was drunk in the spirit! You know, the feeling you have when you don't want it to go away, and you wish you could bottle it up and keep it."

Saved Sister said, "Girl, I know just what you're talking about. Sheila, maybe this singles meeting will turn out to be where you'll find your future husband. Sheila, you just have got to trust God."

With that, they sat and talked some more for a while, then prayed. As she was getting ready to leave, Saved Sister said, "Honey, you really should come to this meeting; it will do you good to get out and mingle with people."

That night, Sheila sat on her bed for a time, and thought again about the thunderclaps and the dancing things at work and at the mall. Then, gazing upwards, she asked, "Lord, what does it all mean? I don't understand any of it. Are you trying to tell me something, Lord? If so, what is it? Please tell me."

CHAPTER TWO
GOD IS TRYING TO TELL HER SOMETHING

Before she climbed into bed for the night, Sheila fervently recited the same prayer she had been saying for so long: "Please, Lord. Bless me with a husband who loves You with all his heart; and who will love me the way that You intend for a husband to love his wife."

No sooner had she finished her prayer, when Sheila experienced the strong feeling that God was about to do something. Sheila then began praising God, because she believed that what God was about to do was to send her the husband of her prayers, and her dreams.

Later that week, on the day before the church singles meeting, Saved Sister called Sheila and asked her if she was going to go. Sheila answered, "Why not?" Saved Sister then told Sheila she would pick her up the next day at about six o'clock in the evening.

The next day, Saved Sister drove Sheila to the church. When they arrived at the singles meeting, Sheila immediately noticed that a large number of people were in attendance, and thought to herself, *Wow! Look at all these people wanting to meet someone!* Sheila hadn't expected the church to be filled with so many people. This made her feel a bit uneasy, as she had never liked large crowds.

Shortly after she and Saved Sister walked in, a handsome man with a nice smile caught Sheila's eye. When they did the mingle rotations, he came up to her and they introduced themselves. Sitting down together, they talked for a while. As Sheila began to get to know him, she couldn't believe how much they had in common. One thing that made a strong impression on her was that he was a minister.

Her face began to turn very red, because she was blushing. She just *knew* that this man was *him*. Mr.Right. Noticing her red hue, he asked, "Why are you turning so red in the face, girl?"

Putting up a front, Sheila responded, "Oh, my face just does this when I smile a lot."

After a while, the mingle rotation came up again, and with regret Sheila thought, *Dang!*

Over the course of the evening, Sheila met a number of men, some interesting, some really strange. But *there* was one who just got on her nerves. He was so fine — tall and dark, like a smooth Dove chocolate bar. He had a perfect smile and perfect white teeth; and Sheila just loved it when a man had perfect white teeth. She sensed that he was a ladies' man; but she didn't care because she just knew she already found her Mr.Right. The only downside was that all of the other women present were looking at him as well.

During the last mingle rotation of the meeting, Sheila heard the thunderclap again. But this time, it was louder than ever. Then, looking around, Sheila saw that all of the men had the spinning *things* on their heads. One of the things appeared to be on fire, while a couple of others looked like they were hanging on the sides of the men's heads or something. The whole scene was amazing to Sheila. Noticing the puzzled expression on her face, and sensing that she was a bit shaken up about something, the man she was with asked, "Are you all right?"

"Yes, I'm fine," she answered, sounding a bit distracted.

"Can I get you a glass of water?"

"No, thank you. Really, I'm fine. Just a little tired."

As the meeting neared its conclusion, Sheila could not get her mind off the minister. She knew he was the man for her, the very one she had been praying for night after night. She firmly believed that God had finally answered her prayers; and if anyone had tried to tell her otherwise, she would have dismissed them.

As the night neared its end, the other women were all over Sheila's man of God. However, in the midst of all this attention, he glanced in her direction a couple of times, and Sheila knew that he was looking at *her*.

But the minister wasn't the only man there attracting major attention. The women were also going nuts over a second man, a man whom Sheila called in her mind "Mr. Pretty Boy." As Sheila and another lady stood looking him over, Sheila said, "I have to admit he's fine. But he looks like drama to me." Noticing her looking at him, Mr. Pretty Boy began looking at Sheila as well, which made her uncomfortable. Soon, she totally dismissed him by not paying any attention to him at all.

At one point Mr. Pretty Boy began walking towards Sheila, and she immediately turned and made a beeline for the ladies room to avoid him. By now Sheila had her heart firmly set on the minister, on Mr. Right and she didn't want Mr. Pretty Boy or anyone or anything to get in the way.

On the way home, Sheila eagerly asked Saved Sister, "When will the next singles meeting be?"

Saved sister replied, "Girl, you must have gotten lucky."

"Yeah, girl! I think I've found my husband! I can feel it in my bones!"

That night at home, Sheila was so happy she just started giving God all the glory, saying, "Lord, I thank you

8

in advance for I know in my heart that I have found him. Lord, I have faith that you are going to send him to me."

Later, in bed, Sheila was too excited to sleep. Picking up her Bible, she started to read. As she did, her attention was drawn to **Hebrews 11:6**:

> But without faith it is impossible to please God, for he who comes to God must believe that He Is, and that. He is a rewarder of those who diligently seek HIM.

Sheila suddenly experienced a vision of the things spinning above the men's heads. But now, instead of appearing as confusing shapes, she could clearly see them as though they were on a freeze frame. To Sheila, it appeared as though the things were *crowns*, gold in color, hovering over their heads. One man had fire over his hovering crown.

At this, Sheila said, "Lord, what does this mean? I know I'm not going crazy. Lord, I know that you are mighty and awesome, and I believe in your supernatural power, unlike some people who don't believe or understand. But Lord, I do. Lord, I know that you hear my prayers and that you know my heart. Have your way in my life, Lord; that's all that I can say. I trust you, Lord, and I give you your glory in advance."

After falling asleep, Sheila had a dream in which she saw the men's faces. Some of them had peaceful expressions, but something was missing. They were not happy. Some were angry; some were sad; and one had an expression of pure evil.

Only one of the men was smiling and appeared happy and whole and at peace. Something else that distinguished him from the others was that his crown was not spinning and hovering over his head, but was resting squarely on his head.

When Sheila awoke the next morning, she could vividly remember her dream. "Lord, what in the world do those crowns above those men's heads mean? And were those things above the men's heads at my job and at the mall crowns as well? Is that what they were? Lord, I believe that you are trying to tell me or show me something, and I'm going to put myself in a place where I can hear from you. I am going to fast and pray."

Finishing her fast a couple of days later, Sheila went to visit her best friend, Nollie, whom she had known since the two had been children. They had gone all the way from kindergarten through college together.

Nollie was a down-to-earth, direct person who said whatever she felt. With Nollie, what you saw was what you

10

got. Although not saved, she did believe in Jesus, and respected Sheila's life as being a women of God. Sheila prayed for Nollie, but allowed her to be herself.

As they sat and talked in Nollie's house, Nollie abruptly broke down and said, "Girl, I'm tired of living like this. I think Adam is seeing somebody else."

"Besides you and his wife?" asked Sheila.

"Yeah, Girl. I know you disagree with me living as a mistress like this. But Adam's so generous. He gave me this house. He gave me that Cadillac outside. And he gives me and our baby so much. But you know what? I'm getting tired of living like this, being with a married man. I want to get out of this relationship and get myself a job. There's nothing I can do about me having had his baby; what's done is done. Sheila, I have prayed and asked God to forgive me. I am so tired of this. I deserve better."

"Amen!" exclaimed Sheila. "Girl, you DO deserve better! And I'm so proud of you for aspiring for a better life for yourself." Continuing, she said, "Girl, I went to this church singles meeting with Saved Sister not long ago. There were so many men there, I couldn't believe it, and they were really fine, too. In fact I found one myself; he just doesn't know it yet."

Nollie said, "Am I hearing you right? Saying you've found yourself a man and that he's fine and all that stuff? That's not the Sheila I know!"

At this they both starting laughing, then Sheila said, "Oh yes, Girl, you're hearing me right! And I can't wait to go back to the next meeting this Friday. You know, Nollie, you should come with me just for the fun of it. You need to get out of the house and get your mind off Adam."

"You know what, Sheila? If it's that meeting that's making you talk about finding a man and all, then I've got to go to the next one with you to see what it's all about."

Sheila replied. "Girl, you've got nothing to lose. After all, there's nothing else out here."

On Thursday, the day before the next singles meeting, Sheila called Nollie. "Girl, you all ready for tomorrow?"

"Sure!" Nollie said.

"Great! Saved Sister and I will stop by and pick you tomorrow evening at six."

The next evening, as Saved Sister and Sheila stepped into Nollie's living room, Sheila saw that Nollie clothes she was wearing left little to the imagination.

"Nollie now remember, girl, this is a church we're going to, not a nightclub," said Sheila. "So go put something

12

else on! Show up wearing that, and you'll have all those men ready to commit sin!"

Chiming in, Saved Sister said, "Lord Jesus, girl! Yes, hurry up and change!"

They all busted into laughter.

"All right, girls. I should have known you wouldn't have any of it." So saying, Nollie changed into more modest attire, and they left for the church.

No sooner had they arrived at the meeting and walked into the church, when Mr. Pretty Boy spotted Sheila and began walking towards her. *Oh, boy! Here we go!* Sheila thought to herself. She wanted to say to him, "Baby, you can just hang it up because I'm going to get my husband to be tonight! And your not him!" but she kept those words to herself.

CHAPTER THREE
GOD HAS A SENSE OF HUMOR

So here they were, having just arrived at the meeting, and Sheila could hardly wait to see her Mr. Right, whom she had learned name was Brother Fred. But now Mr. Pretty Boy, whose real name was Kenny, was in her way, literally, talking about how he wanted to take her out for some coffee.

*He needs to get out of my way so I can get to my **man** — the man I've always believed that God would send to me!* Sheila thought, trying to hide her anxiety and irritation. *I need to get over to my man!*

So, Sheila excuses herself to the restroom and when she returned, Sheila's anxiety turned to alarm when she returned and saw her friend Nollie standing with Brother Fred and pretty boy— and she was writing down *her* phone number!

*Oh My God! Nollie has got to be nuts if she thinks she's about to get my **man**!* thought Sheila in shock. *After all of my praying, crying, whining, and fasting, I don't think so!* And then Sheila thought about how God has such a sense of humor. Only right now, she wasn't laughing.

Finally, after some mingling with some more people, Sheila and Brother Fred were standing together finally able to talk to one another.

"Are you enjoying yourself?" asked Sheila.

"Yes, I'm having a wonderful time," he replied.

"Have you met anyone interesting?" Sheila listened closely for his answer.

"Yeah, I've met a few people. And what about you?"

Sheila said, "Actually, I've only met one person who's caught my attention; and he stole the show and I'm good if it was left up to me."

"Oh really?" he responded.

"Yes!" Sheila said firmly.

"May I ask who?" he asked.

And wouldn't you know it — before she could give him the answer, Mr. Pretty Boy, flashing his pearly whites, sidled up and said, "Excuse me," to Brother Fred. Then, turning to Sheila, Mr. Pretty Boy continued, "Now, back to what we were talking about…"

Before Sheila could tell him how rude he is being, Tanya walked up to Brother Fred, and started to engage Brother Fred in conversation. As the two spoke, they walked off.

Feeling like her chance with Brother Fred, was starting to slip through her fingers, Sheila turned fire-engine red; there was no concealing her anger now. Seeing that she was obviously upset for some reason, Mr. Pretty Boy jokingly said, "Girl, if you don't calm yourself down, you'll blow a gasket. What in the world's wrong, child? Are you angry at me for interrupting you?"

As tactfully as she could manage, Sheila replied, "Well, to be quite frank with you, I'm a little disappointed that he just walked away."

Mr. Pretty Boy then asked, "Can I take you out for coffee one of these days when your normal color comes back to your face?" All Sheila could do was laugh.

Then Mr. Pretty Boy continued, saying something that caught Sheila totally by surprise because it came from him. "Calm down. Everything will be all right. Just remember: What God has for you, it's for you."

Sheila said, "You're right,".

Looking up, Sheila saw Mr. Right with Nollie again, the two looking like they were enjoying each other's company. *Oh my God! And I brought her to this meeting! This is too much! I'm ready to go. I can't believe they exchanged numbers!* thought Sheila in dismay.

In the car, on the way home, Sheila couldn't help but hear Nollie going on and on about Brother Fred, how nice he was — and how she could see herself going out with him. And how she was going to *get him*.

Although mad as ever, Sheila did her best to refrain from speaking. Finally, however, she simply couldn't hold it in any longer. "Look!" she snapped. "Brother Fred is a man of God! So don't go playing any games with him! If that's your idea, then just give him to me!"

Surprised at Sheila's outburst, Saved Sister said, "Sheila! Girl, I can't believe your acting like this!"

Sheila said, "I can't help it! Besides, Nollie already has a man!"

Nollie said, "Girl, I know he's a man of God and also the youth Pastor. He's a really nice man, and I plan to get to know him better. Besides, what are you complaining for? You had the finest guy in there. All of those pretty white teeth. All the women were checking him out, but he was following you around like a sick puppy. All the women were talking about him and how they all wanted his number."

Sheila said, "That was not the man I had my heart set on. But he did tell me this: What God has for me, it is for me."

Looking at Sheila in surprise, Saved Sister said, "Mr. Pretty Boy actually said that? He must be some kind of man, because you know how men are. They can be prideful. But he sounds like he must be an all right guy! I don't even know him, but I think I like him already."

CHAPTER FOUR
"HOW DID YOU GET MY NUMBER?"

The moment Sheila arrived home, her phone rang.

"Hello?"

"Hi, Sheila. This is Kenny, from the singles meeting."

Mr. Pretty Boy! gasped Sheila inwardly. "How did you get my number?" she asked.

"I begged your friend Nollie for it."

"So, Kenny, what's up?"

"Well…when I saw you, Sheila, my heart just soared. Never in my life have I ever beheld a woman who caused me to react like that."

"Oh, really?" replied Sheila.

"Yeah. I know you don't know me, but you are just so naturally beautiful, without a lot of makeup. I'm not sure how to say this, but there's just something special about you."

"Why, thank you," Sheila couldn't help but be flattered by his compliment.

"So…can we go out for coffee?" he asked.

Sheila demurred that time. But after that they continued talking by phone regularly. Finally, two weeks later, she agreed to go out with him for coffee.

During the date, Kenny made an extraordinary admission to Sheila:

"I've been praying every day for God to help me find a virtuous woman. I'd been going to those singles meetings for weeks, but never met the kind of woman I was looking for. And then I saw you. And the instant I did, it was like God pricked my heart and said, 'There she is, the one you've been praying for'. Sheila, I don't know how to describe it, but it was like you were an angel or something. Honey, you can't imagine the number of nights that I've been praying for a woman of God.

"Those other women at the meetings just weren't women of God, and they weren't looking for the same kind of person I've been looking for. Everywhere I go, women try to talk to me. I know I'm a handsome man, but I'm also a man of integrity, and I honor God. There have even been times when women have tried to get me to fornicate with them. And when I tell them no, they just say that I'm gay. But you know what I do? I speak the Word of God to them, and that knocks them on their butts. Sheila, it messes them up every time. I know it sounds lame to say the word 'fornicate,' but that's exactly what they're after. So I've just about given up even trying to be friends with women.

"There was this one young lady I used to go to the movies and hang out with, until she started tripping so I just stopped dealing with her. Then I started going to those church singles meetings, praying to find a woman of God — a woman who could see beyond my looks.

"And then God sent you — even though you'd barely give me the time of day! I've never been so ignored in all my life!"

At this, both Sheila and Kenny laughed. Then Kenny continued, "Sheila, after that meeting when I first saw you, I got home and said, 'Lord, that's her! Thank you God! I know that she is going to be my wife! I could feel it in my heart!' The way I felt, it was as if God told me that you were the women for me."

Having listened intently to what Kenny had revealed, Sheila realized that they had been asking God for the very same thing — that they had been praying every day for their soul mate. At this realization, Sheila felt a lump in her throat and tried to fight back her tears. But she couldn't, and so she just sat there, listening to Kenny in complete attention, with tears streaming down her face.

"Sheila, at the meetings you had me nervous for a while. God knows what is best for us, and He knows our hearts' desires. Even when we think that we know, it is God who truly knows what's best. After all, He knows all things. Honey, you just *knew* that Brother Fred was the man for you; but God knew differently. Sheila, after that second meeting, I thought to myself, *Oh, no, Brother Fred, you're not getting* ***this*** *one!* That night, as soon as I got home, I just started quoting every scripture I could find about the Righteousness of God.

"**Psalm 37:4** *Delight yourself also in the Lord, and he will give you the desires of your heart.*

"**Matthew 6:33** *Seek ye first the kingdom of heaven and its righteousness and all things shall be added unto you.*

"Then I said, 'Lord, you said that this woman is her, and I believe you that she is to be mine.' And it was right after that when I decided to take the risk of calling you. I know you could have told me to get lost, and hung up on me. But I just acted on faith that everything was going to be all right."

After Kenny finished telling Sheila what he had been praying and believing God for, she literally wanted to run around the coffee shop screaming with joy because she knew that God doesn't make any mistakes, He knows all things.

At home later that night, alternately laughing and crying, Sheila fell to her knees and said, "God, you heard and answered me! Lord, you know I love me some chocolate, and you gave me a Dove Bar Daddy! This man is so fine! I love you so much, Lord! There is none like you on all of the earth!"

Later that week, on a vacation day from work, Sheila patched things up over the phone with Nollie, then went over to Nollie's house for lunch. As they sat and talked, Nollie began to tell Sheila about Brother Fred. She told Sheila how nice he was to her; and that she had told him about her baby's daddy, Adam, and the fact that he was a married man, and how she wanted to get out of the relationship.

Nollie continued, "Girl, even after telling Brother Fred all of that, he didn't criticize me or treat me any different. He's so different from Adam. In fact, Adam's been tripping lately, and he's stopped doing anything for me and our baby. I've stopped sleeping with Adam. And since then, he doesn't come around that much. All he does is come over sometimes, gets the baby and they leave for a while. Girl, I even said to him about a year ago to leave his wife and marry me, or it's over. But you know what? Since I've been talking to Brother Fred, my heart's been changing. He's been ministering to me, showing me things in the Bible I didn't even realize were there. Like, I don't have a right to ask God for somebody else's husband. It's amazing how God works in mysterious ways. Sheila, I was just telling you how I wanted to stop seeing Adam and get a job. Now I know that when we pray, God hears us. Now I'm going to believe in Him for a job so I can pay these bills."

"Amen, Nollie," Sheila smiled. "I stand in agreement with you that God is going to bless you with good a job."

CHAPTER FIVE
REAL LOVE FINALLY COMES

"Enough about me," said Nollie. "What about you and Kenny? What have y'all been up to?"

"Oh, nothing girl," answered Sheila with a big Kool-Aid smile on her face.

"Girl, you look so happy," Nollie said, then started to tear up and gave Sheila a big hug.

"Nollie, don't go starting that crying stuff, girl!"

"Sheila, you know how long I've been waiting to see you happy? Girl, let's go on a double date to the movies this week end. Kenny and you, Brother Fred and I We will have a good time. That way, I can give him my stare-down"

They both started laughing, and Sheila jokingly said, "Nollie, what we gonna do if Brother Fred and Kenny are playing? Hit 'em in the head with something?"

"Girl, I just know that they're not playing. Sheila, Kenny offered to give me money for your phone number. And, girl, that money looked so good. But I said to him, 'If you're willing to pay for my sisters' phone number, you must be serious.' And I'll tell you, girl, he just had this look on his face like calling you was a life-or-death matter for him. He was so serious. It was different from guys in the street who have no good intentions. Sheila, I just have the feeling that this man's going to be your husband. I don't know why, but that's just what I felt when I was writing your number down for him. Then I thought, 'She is so lucky.' I mean, I wanted to cry, it was such a weird but good feeling."

"Yeah, Nollie. Yes, Kenny will be my husband."

At this, Nollie started dancing and snapping her fingers, chanting repeatedly, "Sheila's getting a husband! Sheila's getting a husband!"

Then Sheila jumped up and started dancing, saying, "Thank you, Lord, for my husband!"

For several minutes they laughed and danced around like two kids. Finally Nollie said, "Oh, Sheila. My sweetie's told me about this great movie. That's what we could go see on our double date."

Just as Nollie finished speaking, Adam suddenly walked in the door.

Sheila said, "Hey, Adam."

He replied, "Hey, Sheila."

Then Sheila suddenly heard the loud thunderclap again; and as Adam walked past, she saw a gold thing hanging over his head, but leaning lopsided to the left, just as clear as day. *Oh, Lord*, Sheila thought to herself.

Noticing Sheila's strange expression, Adam asked, "Are you all right?"

"Yeah, I'm OK."

"By the way, Sheila, are you and Brother GTM (Get That Money) — Dwayne — cousins?"

"Yeah, you know him?"

"Yeah. We played ball together."

Sheila was puzzled. *I have never in my entire life seen Dwayne with a ball*, thought Sheila to herself. Presently, realizing it was time to go home, Sheila told Nollie she would give her a call later.

As soon as she returned home, Sheila got on her computer and started to look up the meaning of "crowns." After a while, she came across the following Biblical scriptures:

Psalms 21:1 THE king shall have joy in your strength, O Lord: And in Your salvation how greatly shall he rejoice!

Psalms 21:2 You have given him his hearts desire. And have not withheld the request of his lips. Selah.

Psalms 21:3 For you meet him with the blessings of goodness. You set a crown of pure gold on his head.

Sheila was excited over learning at last the significance of the crowns. Continuing her search, she

29

uncovered a few more scriptures that referenced Crowns and pure Gold.

CHAPTER SIX
THE BOOK AUTHOR

Continuing her online search, Sheila came across a book titled, *The Krown of Men*. Reading the details of the book, she found that the author, Mother Banks, was a local Christian woman. After reading summaries and reviews of the book, Sheila realized that it was imperative she meet Mother Banks. To this end, she located Mother Banks' contact information, called her, and asked if she could talk to her concerning her book. After speaking briefly, During their phone conversation, with Sheila. Mother Banks then asked Sheila a few questions, and invited Sheila to come over to her home.

Arriving at Mother Banks' home on the appointed day, Sheila was immediately impressed with it; the home was a very nice ranch-style condo, and it was immaculate.

After exchanging introductions, Mother Banks invited Sheila inside. Immediately Sheila found Mother Banks to be a warm and pleasant woman.

In the living room, Mother Banks invited Sheila to have a seat, and then Sheila related her story again, but in greater detail than she had over the phone.

Finished with her narrative, Sheila said, "I know you probably think I'm strange, but your book is the only thing that makes sense to me right now."

After asking Sheila some more questions, Mother Banks said, "Sheila, you are a chosen vessel from God. You have a special gift from God. And now, if I may, let me tell you about my own life."

So saying, Mother Banks related how, just like Sheila, she had prayed every day for God to send her a loving husband, a gentle man of God. As she told her story, tears ran down both her and Sheila's faces. Mother Banks had the very same desire that Sheila did.

However, Mother Banks revealed, she had never found her husband. Sheila said she understood, Mother Banks then said how she had ultimately told God, "If it is not in Your Will for me to get married, then I accept that and will dedicate my life to serving You and being a vessel for You."

Mother Banks went on to explain the meaning of the crowns, and how God chooses certain people to serve as vessels for the body of Christ. God had shown her things about people in such a way that they would know that only God could have told her. He gave her a gift of prophecy Along with this special gift. She said to Sheila, "You must be a very special person to God. But you must also know that this gift from God will require a lot of you. God is so awesome and so deep that you should not try to figure Him out or second-guess Him when He tells you to do something. Just do it. What God may ask you to do might seem strange or out of order, but you must *trust* Him."

Opening her Bible, Mother Banks then read to Sheila the following scripture:

"Isaiah 55:9 For as the heavens are higher in the earth. So are my ways, higher than your ways, and my thoughts than your thoughts. ""

When she finished, Mother Banks said, "Praise God."

Mother Banks went on to tell Sheila that she had been waiting for a long time to be able to talk to someone face-to-face about this wonderful gift from God. "Many people would think you are crazy if you told them that all men are very special to God, and that they are born with crowns over their heads that only God see — crowns positioned on their heads to reflect their lifestyles. Sheila, I have seen some things so heartbreaking that I could never share them with anyone else but God. Just know that the two of us are very special to God; and He gave us this ability, this gift, of being able to see the crowns because He knows that

He can trust us with it. Do you understand what I'm telling you? You have been chosen by God. But you must never reveal this unless He wills you to do so."

As their visit drew to a close, Mother Banks gave Sheila a copy of *The Krown of Men*, telling her that it contained all of the information that she needed to know. As Mother Banks opened the door to see Sheila out, she offered the following parting words: "Sheila, your life is about to change dramatically. God is about to use you for something very special. It won't be easy at times. But if you ever need to talk, if you ever feel overwhelmed, please call me anytime."

Leaving Mother Banks' house, Sheila felt uplifted, as though she were living in a vibrant new body. She was so happy to have finally found someone with whom she could discuss her *gift*, someone who fully understood what it was all about. As soon as she arrived home, Sheila opened the book, read for a time, learned the meaning of the crowns, and then just sat and wept.

Sheila thought about all the crowns she had seen, in particular the one on Adam, the father of Nollie's baby. Discerning the meaning of Adam's crown, based on the book's information, Sheila gasped and thought, *Oh my God,* *he's **gay!*** This revelation forced her to rush into the bathroom, where she threw up.

Looking up the meaning of the spinning crowns she had seen on the men in her workplace, she found that those crowns indicated that the men were wealthy, and were living double lives. With their fancy cars and the airs they put on, they all appeared to be respectable. But they lusted for money and power, and cheated to obtain both. In addition, those who were married also cheated on their wives. Thinking about how they all seemed very arrogant and selfish, Sheila now understood the reasons why.

CHAPTER SEVEN
THE DOOR BELL RINGS

As Sheila sat reading, the phone rang. It was Kenny, who said, "Hey, Hon, what's up? A minute ago, I just had the feeling that I should pray for you and call you. Are you OK?"

"Yeah," Sheila said unconvincingly.

"Are you sure?"

"Actually, Kenny, no I'm not OK."

"I'll be right over."

When he arrived, Sheila heard the doorbell — followed immediately thereafter by the thunderclap sound. Startled, she quickly opened the door, and saw the crown attached to Kenny's head. Dissolving into tears, she grabbed him and hugged him tightly.

"Honey, what in the world is wrong?" his worried face reflected his concern.

Sitting down together on the sofa, Sheila and Kenny held one another, and Kenny began to pray in the Spirit and cry out to God. So strong was God's anointing in the apartment that both found themselves on their knees, crying out to God.

Presently, Kenny stood up and helped Sheila to her feet, then said with passion, "Lord, I just want to thank you for this precious woman of God. Lord, on this day I vow to you that whatever Your Will is for her life, I support it with all of my heart. Lord, I promise not to get in the way. You know my heart, Lord, so please search it now. If there is anything in it that is not to Your liking, then please take it out, God. Lord, I know you sent this woman of God to me, to be just for me, and I also realize that she is a precious vessel."

With that, Kenny fell back down to his knees and continued to pray in the Spirit. As he did so, it was abundantly clear to Sheila just how much he loved and honored God. Just looking at the wonderful man of God before her, Sheila felt like she was floating on a cloud. It was as though he had become totally transparent before her and God.

To both Sheila and Kenny, it felt like the Lord was right there in the apartment with them. Sheila had never in her life met a man who prayed to God as Kenny was doing, who prayed with such a true love for God. Crying with joy, Sheila crying just in awe thinking of the nights that she prayed for this very moment, *Lord, this man loves You so much — just the way I've always imagined that my husband will. Lord, this is exactly what I've been asking and praying to you for.*

After Kenny had finished praying and crying out to God. He and Sheila held each other tight, as tears continued streaming down Sheila's face. Tenderly brushing away one of her tears, Kenny asked, "Honey are you OK?"

"Yes, Kenny. Now I really am OK. I am just so happy. I thank God for sending you to me."

After washing away their tears of sorrow that turned into tears of joy. Sheila started laughing and couldn't stop. Her laughter was contagious, because Kenny started laughing, too. Finally he said, "Baby, God is about to do something!" In response, Sheila shook her head in complete agreement. She couldn't speak, though, because she was still laughing so hard that she couldn't get any words out.

Presently, the phone rang. It was Nollie, who asked if she and Kenny wanted to go and get something to eat at The Lobster with her and Brother Fred. It sounded like a great idea to both Sheila and Kenny, so Sheila told Nollie that they would meet her and Brother Fred at the restaurant in half an hour.

As she hung up the phone, Kenny walked up to her and hugged her without saying a word. Sheila sighed, feeling at long last like she could finally stop tensing herself inside, as she had long done as a defense against men. Feeling herself relaxing internally was like a tremendous weight being lifted off of her body. As he continued to hold her, he said, "I am going to love all of your past hurt away."

Gazing lovingly up at Kenny through her tear-filled eyes, as he tenderly kissed her forehead, Sheila thought, *Lord, I am sorry but I can't wait until my honeymoon!*

CHAPTER EIGHT
THE CONFESSION

"I've known Brother Fred for a while, and he's a pretty nice guy," said Kenny.

"Yes, I know." Replied Sheila.

"I'll bet you wanted to kick me to the curb when you thought I was butting in and preventing you from seeing him at those meetings?" Kenny smiled.

"Honey, I'm not going to lie to you. I was really digging Brother Fred," Sheila admitted. Then she continued, "Kenny, I have to tell you something. I need you to sit down for a minute."

"What is it?"

Taking a deep breath, Sheila said, "I had been praying to God for years, and I believed that He would send a man of God into my life. When I first met Brother Fred, it was like I just *knew* that he was the one for me. He was a man of God, first and foremost, and we also had so much in common." With a smile, she continued, "But you and your persistent little self just wouldn't leave me alone to save my life!" Leaning over and kissing Kenny, Sheila added, "You can't imagine how you were getting on my nerves. In fact, at the church I had thought to myself, *Just look at him with all those pretty white teeth! You have a beautiful smile!* and the fact you are fine, all those women there were checking you out. I thought you were about as serious about me as The Man on the Moon.

"I just had the feeling you were a ladies man, and that you were at the meetings just trying to get your groove on. When you interrupted me and Brother Fred, I think I'd have shot you if I'd had a gun. I just *knew* he was *my man*.

"But God knows what's best for us, including when we are righteous before Him. He hears our prayers, and He knows our true hearts' desires even when we don't. So, I probably would have got with Brother Fred, and maybe ended up as bored as ever. Until getting to know you, I would have never thought you were the man God had chosen for me. Kenny, you are everything I could have asked for, and more. Maybe that's why I ignored you at first. Maybe I felt inside that you were too good to be true.

"But then you said something to me that changed everything. You said, 'What God has for me it is for me.' The instant you said that, my mind turned away from Brother Fred. Later, I just told Nollie to treat him right because he is a man of God.

"When you told me how you had been praying and asking the Lord to send you a virtuous women of God, a women for you to love, a woman who would love you back the way she is supposed to according to God's Word, a woman able to love with the *agape* love of God, it took everything in my power not to run around that Coffee shop. I wanted to chew my lip off, but I wanted to be sure you weren't just playing with me."

Her eyes tearing up again, Sheila continued, "My heart was beating so hard it felt like it was going to jump out of my chest. Honey, I thank God that you were persistent. If I had missed out on you, I never would have known that I could be this happy. You are everything that I have asked for, and so much more."

Kenny said, "Baby, you haven't seen anything yet, because I am going to be so good to you. Your toes are going to curl up when you see me coming."

At this Sheila jumped and said, with a laugh, "Boy! You better not be playing with me!"

"Baby, I know there are men out there who play a lot of games with women of God. I know that most of those women just want a man of God; and men see them as being vulnerable. Some men say, 'Yeah, I love the Lord,' and they know God's Word, too! But they have an agenda. I've talked to some brothers, and they've described some of the games they play with women. The Devil comes in sheep's clothing." Then, an expression of realization coming to his face, he continued, "So is that what was wrong, Sheila? Is that why you wouldn't give me the time of day at first?"

"Kenny nodded, "I figured you were acting standoffish because you didn't think my intentions were honorable."

"That's right," Sheila sighed, looking at him in tears. "I didn't trust you. I've been so deeply hurt by men. And I realized that the only way I would ever find my love is if God sent him to me. So that's why I prayed to God for him every night for so long."

With that Sheila rose, walked to her desk, opened a drawer, and took out her journal. Opening the journal, she showed Kenny her entries chronicling all of the days and nights she had prayed to God to send her a man who loved God and who would love her just the same.

"Kenny, I hadn't felt loved in so many years that I forgot what it felt like for a man to really love me. But when I finally realized that God loves me, He took all of that hurt away. I realized that His love is the best love I will ever get. Because His love doesn't judge you or hurt you, it just pours down on you. Baby, it feels so good because it is genuine and pure *agape* love. Praise God!"

At this, Kenny wept softly for several minutes. Finally he said, "Baby, I'm sorry for crying so much, but with the joy that I feel, I can't help but cry. God has given me, blessed me with, *you* —a virtuous woman. I promise to never hurt you or judge you. I promise to always love you and support you. It's amazing how the Lord works. We were both saying the same prayer to God, probably at the same times, and believing that He would answer our prayers — and now here we are together. This has to have been divinely ordered by God. Honey, I feel like we've known each other for years. I feel as though I'm already a part of you, and you a part of me."

With that he grabbed Sheila and hugged her so tight she could barely breathe. In a squeaky voice she smiled and said, "Okay, baby! It's OK! You *got* me! I'm not going anywhere! Oh, and I can't breathe, either!" At this they both started laughing. Finally Sheila said, "Come on, let's go eat. I'm hungry."

Kenny smiled and said. "All right, baby. But look! You have to promise not to tell anybody about all my crying. Unless, of course, God tells you to."

At The Lobster, seeing Nollie and Brother Fred together, Sheila felt a little awkward, remembering how much she had wanted him. But Sheila was so happy for both

Nollie and Brother Fred, because they both seemed so happy in each other's company.

Sheila said, "Man, I was just thinking about our lives of a few months ago. I would have never thought that I would be as happy as I am right now. There is so much love coming from this table. Praise God! Hallelujah!"

They all laughed and said "Amen!"

Later, after having a blast with Nollie and Brother Fred, as Kenny drove Sheila home, he said, "Honey, I'd like you to meet my parents tomorrow. I want to take you to their place so we can have lunch with them."

"Kenny, I'd love to meet your parents. I was beginning to think you were hiding me from them, like I was the ugly duckling or something," she teased. "It's about time you brought me around to somebody you know."

Kenny laughed and said, "Girl, you are so silly!"

Walking Sheila up to her front door a few minutes later, Kenny kissed her passionately.

CHAPTER NINE

KENNY INTRODUCES SHEILA TO HIS PARENTS

When Kenny picked Sheila up the next day, he looked admiringly at her and said, "Wow, honey, you look really nice!"

"Why thank you. This is my favorite sun dress. You look very nice, too."

On the way to Kenny's parent's home, Kenny told Sheila how his parents had been Christians all their lives. He said, "I never heard them curse or saw them drink. They've always lived their lives for God."

When they arrived at his parent's house, Sheila was surprised at how large it was. She was also impressed that it featured a circular driveway. *Wow!* Sheila thought to herself, then said to Kenny, "Honey, your parents certainly have a nice home."

"Yes, I've always loved it. This is the house I grew up in."

After he rang the doorbell to let his parents know that he and Sheila had arrived, he unlocked the front door and they entered. "Ma! Dad! We're here!" he called out.

When they entered the family room, they found that Kenny's parents were watching a movie. Kenny hugged his mother and hugged his father. Then, smiling, he said to them, "I'd like to introduce you to my friend, Sheila."

Shaking their hands warmly, Sheila said, "I'm very pleased to meet you."

"I have lunch ready; let's go into the dining room," invited Kenny's mother, and the four sat down for lunch. Sheila asked which way is the wash room?

Kenny point and said just down the hall. Kenny's parents whispered she is adorable.

Kenny's father said Grace, then they began their meal.

"So tell me, Sheila, how you guys met?" asked Kenny's mother.

"We met at one of the church singles meetings."

Kenny chimed in and said," Ma, you won't believe this, but before we met we were both praying to God and asking Him for the very same thing: A God-loving mate."

Looking at Kenny, Sheila smiled and said, "No crying for me today, honey."

Turning to her husband, Kenny's mother said, "Dear, do you see that?"

"I certainly do."

Puzzled, Kenny asked, "What, Ma? What do you see?"

She said, "You guys have a glow coming from you. You're the same way your dad and I were when we first met. We loved each other so much that we just knew God had brought us together. We knew in our hearts that we were meant to be together."

With a twinkle in his eye, Kenny's father turned to Sheila and said, "Please pass the salad — daughter."

Returning his smile, Sheila replied, "Yes, sir."

"Did she just say 'Yes, sir' to me?"

Sheila said, "I hope I didn't offend you. A lot of people don't like it when I say 'Yes, sir' or 'Yes, ma'am' to them; but that's the way I was raised. In my family, if you didn't respect your elders, you'd get a back-hand. So I just can't help it."

"Oh, no, you didn't offend me at all. Quite the opposite, in fact. I was just a bit shocked because you hardly ever hear such expressions of respect from the younger folks. Even the older generation rarely shows such respect these days. Sheila, you are all right with me."

Kenny's mom gave her "seal of approval" by saying, "Welcome to the family, Sheila."

Sitting there, Sheila thought, *What wonderful parents Kenny has! So down to earth, and so funny!*

CHAPTER TEN
SHEILA TELLS HER SISTER TANYA

After her return home from the delightful meeting with Kenny's parents, Sheila went over to her sister Tanya's house to tell her the news of her relationship with Kenny. Sheila would have liked to have told their parents as well; but, sadly, both their mother and father were deceased, and so Tanya was her only sibling but, they had many cousins. They are all very close.

Sheila told Tanya everything — how she had met Kenny, and how she had come to learn that he was exactly the man for whom she had been praying in faith to God.

After hearing the incredible and wonderful news, Tanya was very happy and excited for Sheila. She knew that Sheila had been waiting for years to find a good man.

"Girl, you have a glow of joy all over you! I could see it on your face as soon as you walked in the door! God is good!" said Tanya. Then she had an idea. "Sheila, I want to have a big barbeque for y'all so that all the relatives can meet Kenny. I'll contact everybody and make all the arrangements. It'll be fun!"

"What a wonderful idea!" Sheila replied. "Thank you so much, Tanya!

Looking at her positively glowing sister, Tanya recalled how Sheila had been through a lot of bad relationships with fake and phony guys who had hurt her really bad. But now, knowing that at last her sister had found the man of her dreams and prayers, a good man of God and not just any old man, Tanya's heart was filled with joy! *Praise God!* She thought to herself.

From Tanya's house, Sheila called Mother Banks, the author of *The Krown of Men*, and invited her to the barbecue. Mother Banks responded that she would love to come.

Several hours later, after Sheila had arrived back home, however, her heart started to feel very heavy, as though something was amiss. At first, she merely had the vague sense that something wasn't quite right; but then, in the pit of her stomach, came the feeling that something was wrong. The feeling grew stronger and stronger until finally, looking up, she said, "Lord, what is it? What's wrong? Why am I feeling this way?" That said, she immediately started to pray in the Spirit. As she prayed, the feeling that something was wrong became so intense that she began to cry.

"Lord, I don't know what's happening. But, Lord, You know all things; and so I ask You right now to cover whatever is wrong with Your blood." Continuing to pray in the Spirit, she said, "Lord, I sense that You want me to intercede on someone's behalf. Have Your way, Lord, in the name of Jesus. Lord, I ask that You send Your Angels of Protection to help make right whatever it is that's wrong!"

CHAPTER ELEVEN
THE PHONE CALL

Later that night, the phone rang. Answering it, Sheila was greeted by Tanya's voice; and could immediately sense the worry in her sister's voice.

"I have to tell you something, Sheila. I wanted to wait till after the barbeque, but something told me that I need to tell you now."

"What is it, Tanya? What's wrong?"

"Well…I've got some bad news about our cousin, Dwayne, GTM."

"What has he done, Tanya?"

"Sheila, that boy is so out cold with this gay stuff. He sells his body to anything that's got some money and that's breathing." Tanya took a deep breath, and continued. "I just got the news that he's HIV-Positive. What's more, he knows it, and he's still out on the streets selling his body. I heard he's messing with some guy who's married and has a baby by this other lady. But the guy is undercover, in the closet. He's a macho guy, and you'd never think he's bisexual."

Something about the news — something that sounded *familiar* — struck Sheila in the stomach like a punch. She said, "Girl, what is this guy's name?"

"I don't know, but I'll find out and call you back."

As Sheila awaited Tanya's call, she felt sick with dread. On the one hand, she didn't want to know the guy's name. On the other hand, although she hoped otherwise, she was virtually certain she already knew who he was.

When Tanya called, she confirmed Sheila's worst fears. "Sheila, it is Adam. Nollie's boyfriend."

At this, Sheila's heart just dropped. "Are you sure?"

"Yeah. I'd heard a few rumors that he was bisexual. I just didn't believe it because he doesn't look like he could be that way".

"I know, Sis. Thanks for telling me, baby. I'll be praying."

"Me, too, Sheila. I love you so much."

"I love you, too".

Hanging up the phone, Sheila took a deep breath and remembered the meaning of Adam's crown. She said, "Oh, Lord, you are so powerful. His crown confirmed his lifestyle. In the book it showed him as being gay. Oh my God!"

CHAPTER TWELVE
CHURCH AT THE BARBEQUE

On the day of the barbeque, everyone was there. Tanya had a very large backyard, and she decked it all out; she even had a stage attached to her back patio. All of Sheila's friends, cousins, nieces, nephews, and church members were there. There had to be more than one hundred people present. Stepping onto the stage, Sheila cried and cried as she told everyone how she was blessed to have family members and friends that loved her, and cared enough to show up to celebrate with her. She said, "I just want y'all to know that when you pray, God hears you and He sees your tears. I know, because he saw mine. I also know that He is not partial, but loves us all the same." Then Sheila recited the following scripture:

Acts 10:34 Then peter opened his mouth and said; God shows no partiality.

Continuing, Sheila said, "This is so sweet, and it's such a beautiful day! If I could just stop crying for a minute!"

At this, everyone started laughing in the spirit of good fellowship.

"I want y'all to know that I love each and every one of you." She then told them the story of how she and Kenny had met. When she finished, it seemed as though there wasn't a dry in the back yard; everybody was crying, especially the women.

Moments later, she had them all cracking up when she told them, "At first Kenny seemed like a pesky fly to me, a fly that just kept bothering me and wouldn't go away. Even after I 'swatted' at him a couple of times, he just kept coming back. And now…please let me introduce you to the love of my life. Come up here, honey."

Kenny joined Sheila on the stage, and everyone started clapping and whistling in approval. "Everyone, this is Kenny, the man God gave to me in fulfillment of the blueprint of my heart," Sheila said proudly.

"Thank you all for coming and for honoring Sheila, and me as well. I just want to tell you how grateful I am to God for having sent me this very beautiful woman, a woman of God who is every bit as beautiful on the inside as on the outside."

Pausing, his expression became serious; then he continued. "Now I want to say something to all the brothers here. I want you to know that, just as a woman can pray and believe that God will bring her a good man, so can a man pray and believe that God will bring him a good woman. Let me tell you, brothers, that this lovely woman is the blueprint of everything that I asked of God, and believed He would provide, and more. Sheila is a special woman.

"I know how easy it is to get into that whirlwind where there are many women for one man. But you must remember that whirlwind is not love. What Sheila and I have *is* love, true love. Now, true love is hard to come by. But with God all things are possible. Sheila and I being together is living proof of that. Praise God!

"Because we're in a world where people want what you can give or do for them, it seems like love comes out last on the list, when it should be first. What people don't realize is that when you put love first, everything else will follow. So, I'm going to keep it short, brothers, by telling you that when you're ready for that special women who will complete you, take it to the Lord. Like I said, 'With God all things are possible.' He created a woman just for you — and she's sitting somewhere waiting for you right now."

With that, Kenny jokingly said "let me sit down man, because I am so in love right now. Thank you guys for doing this, I can see this is a family of love thanks" Kenny left the stage and sat down, to the sounds of loud whistling and enthusiastic applause.

"I love you too, honey," she said to Kenny. Then, looking out at all the people, Sheila said, "I just want to finish by saying thank you to every last one of you. Oh, and one last thing. Since all the people that I love are here, it would make me very happy if we could all gather in prayer after we eat."

Sheila looked up and saw her cousin Dwayne comes in. He had this look like he was just tired.

As the barbecue continued, everyone was having a grand time eating, listening to the music that was playing, and doing the Hustle — enjoying themselves in the Lord. Several people came on the stage, where Sheila and Kenny was sitting, and told her how happy they were for her. Then Nollie came up and offered some remarks. At this, She became very emotional. Sheila took her by the arm and said "Come on big cry, baby. After all, you were the main one who was saying, 'I will be glad when you get your husband.' Well, now I got him. So are you happy now?" At this, the two old friends and everyone started laughing, and exchanged a big hug. Sheila said she will be up here for hours telling our childhood stories Then Sheila led her offstage. Everyone laughed again.

Sheila then later called for everyone's attention and said, "Let us all have prayer. Let us come into agreement with one another and believe God in prayer for our hearts' desires according to His will. People don't realize that God know your heart. He sees your tears and he hears your prayers. He loves you so much. Yes, even you. Now listen, seriously you can't go to God and ask him for someone else's spouse; you know what I mean."

Everyone laughed and said "Amen" as they gathered in a circle, held hands, and were ready to pray. Looking out at the crowd, Sheila was startled by the thunderclap sound, after which she could see all kinds of crowns on the heads of the men. *Oh my God in Heaven!* She thought, as she could now interpret the meanings.

Kenny started praying in the Spirit under his breath, but Sheila could hear him. In turn, she began to pray as well, and the Holy Ghost fell upon her. Joining the circle, she began to pray along with the others; and she asked Mother Banks, Brother Fred, Saved Sister, and the other ministers present for their help in praying with everyone.

Kenny continued praying in the Spirit a few minutes into prayer Sheila said, "God has opened a door for somebody right now. Somebody believes in God for a miracle. The doctor said you can't have kids. God says that you shall have a son. If you have something that you want to believe God can bring you, now is the time to pray to Him for that. I am telling you all: You have to trust God right now, while His spirit is right here in this back yard!"

Sheila said, "If you are saved and have the Holy Ghost, please pray in the Spirit right now! If you are not saved, pray anyway. This is serious. The window is open right now. There is no time to be ashamed. If you have something, such as a burden, that you want to give to God, then pray right now for healing and deliverance. Let us pray with you. God knows your hearts and He hears your prayers. Just give it to Him right now. No one here has a secret that God does not already know about. People might not know your secrets, but God knows them, he knows all things. There are no secrets from Him. Please, pray while He is here. Know that He loves you. He wants to heal you, deliver you, and set you free. You have the opportunity to change your lives."

Everyone in the back yard prayed fervently. Sheila notices Adam crying out with his hands raised and she goes over to him and ask him are you ready to give your life to God? He said" Yes yes yes I don't want to live like this no more". Sheila asked him are you tired of being sick and tired he shook his head yes. Sheila said "Adam God has everything you want in life and he loves you so much. She asked him do you believe in your heart that God raised Jesus from the dead ?

Adam said "Yes I do."

Sheila placed her hand on Adams face and said be whole. Suddenly, Sheila heard a swooshing sound as if the Holy Ghost had just entered the yard. Sheila commenced to lay hands on people; and as she did so her hands felt as though they were on fire. Most of those whom she touched immediately fell out. People cried out to God, and Sheila could hear such entreaties as, "Please forgive me, Lord!" Everyone, in their own way, was giving their lives to the Lord. Her hands were still hot, So she laid them on the ministers too. Sheila looked at how the Holy Spirit was moving and said,"Lord have your way!!"

Sheila had never seen or experienced anything so amazing in her entire life. The Glory Cloud was over the entire back yard. It was absolutely awesome. To Sheila, it was abundantly clear that when God said *Move*, Sheila moved! Minutes later, when everyone had finished praying, it seemed to Sheila like three hours had passed.

In effect, Sheila and everyone else had just experienced *church* at a barbeque! For many years, Sheila had dreamed of having everyone close to her in one place so they could all have prayer and accept the Lord into their lives — and now it had happened at last.

Fully realizing what had just happened, the miracle that God had just accomplished, Sheila immediately began praising Him. Everyone else in the back yard immediately followed her lead and began praising Him as well. Even some neighbors, who were peeking over the fence to see what all the commotion was about, some began to praise God right along with them.

Stepping onto the stage, Tanya started singing "Thank You Lord," and everyone else joined in. When Tanya finished, Tanya invited everyone out to church that next Sunday, saying, "It doesn't matter where you are. If you invite the Lord, He will show up."

Suddenly, the sound came. and sheila could see Adams Crown, now over his head. Looking at her cousin Dwayne, she saw that his crown was over his head as well. Going over to Dwayne, Sheila hugged him and said, "God needs you for His Kingdom; he needs you to win souls for the body of Christ. God has also told me to tell you to go to the doctor."

In reply, Dwayne said, "Sheila, I know you've heard the rumor that I'm HIV-Positive. I'll go to the doctor because I have not been to one yet. People are speculating that I have something because I lost so much weight. I lost weight worrying about what they are saying. But on this very day, I believe in my heart that I am healed in the name of Jesus."

"Amen!" said Sheila. "I stand in agreement with you. And I truly want you to remember this: If you don't know anything else in life, know to *trust God*! When He tells you to do something, you do it!"

Sheila hugged Dwayne again, and he broke down and started crying. "Sheila, you're the only family member who loves me. Everybody else just looks down on me."

"That's not true, Dwayne. But if you ever feel like nobody loves you, just know that God loves you with a perfect love. Now, I want you to hear you say, 'God loves me with a perfect love.'"

"God loves me with a perfect love," said Dwayne, and then he just dropped to one knee as though he had been released from a ponderous burden, crying out to God in joy.

In awe of God, Sheila merely whispered, "Thank you, Jesus, for your delivering power."

All of Sheila's immediate family came and began to hug Dwayne and everyone is crying. There was so much emotion from them. It was like love just invaded the back yard.

Dwayne cried and said "I didn't think yawl loved me. But you do, and he just cried." He said" Thank you God. Some men were crying too! God just pulled the cover off of everyone hearts it seems. The anointing was there so strong.

CHAPTER THIRTEEN
DELIVERANCE

Sheila told Dwayne, "Your life has changed, and you will never be the same person again," and recited the following scripture:

Psalms 103:12 As far as the east if from the west. So far hath he redeemed us our transgressions.

"This means," Sheila explained, "that He has forgiven you for your sins, and that He doesn't remember them. So, when the devil brings to your mind thoughts about your past, just laugh and say, 'God has that at Calvary. It does not belong to me.' The devil will try to instill fear in you. Just know that the devil has no authority. The Bible says resist the devil and he will flee. Say, 'I rebuke you, devil, in the name of Jesus.' Dwayne, you can't think it in your mind, you must speak God's word out loud against the enemy. This is how you must guard your mind against the enemy. The Bible says," Sheila continued, reciting the following scriptures:

Psalms 118:17 I shall not die, but live, and declare the works of the Lord.

Psalms 118:18 The Lord has chasten me sore: But he have not given me over to death.

Psalms 118:19 *Open to me the gates of righteousness: I will go into them, and I will praise the Lord:*

Psalms 118:20 *This gate of the Lord, into which the righteous shall enter.*

Psalms 118:21 *I will praise thee for thou has heard me, and art become my salvation.*

Psalms 118:22 *The stone which the builders refused is become the head stone of the corner.*

Psalms 118:23 *This is the Lord's doing; it is marvelous in our eyes.*

Psalms 118:24 *This is the day in which the Lord hath made; we will rejoice and be glad in it.*

Psalms 118:25 *Save now, I beseech thee, O Lord: O Lord, I beseech thee, send now prosperity.*

Psalms 118:28 *Thou art my God, and I will praise thee: thou art my God, I will exalt thee.*

Psalms 118:29 *O give thanks unto the Lord; for he is good: for his mercy endureth forever.*

Psalms 34:4 *I sought the Lord, and he heard me and delivered me from all my fears.*

Psalms 34:7 *The angel of the Lord encampeth round about them that fear him, and delivereth them.*

Psalms 34:8. *O taste and see that the Lord is good: blessed is the man that trusteth in him.*

As Dwayne stood listening in rapt attention, Sheila said.

"you know how I remembered those scriptures? There was a time that I thought I was going to die. I was sick and the doctor's did not know what was wrong with me I had all kinds of test done. I could not hold down food or even water. This went off and on for about six months. So one day my friend came over and she prayed for me in the spirit and I felt better. I thought about it, I said this thing is spiritual thing. From that point I just started to repent for everything that I could think of that I had done wrong to people. I repented for every sin that I could think of. Then I went to people that hurt me and I told them that I forgive them and asked for forgiveness if I had done anything wrong to them. Do you know my sickness left my body? From that point on I grew more and more in love with God and dedicating my life to him. The moment I put my guards down the enemy would put things in my path. There where times I fell, but I got up I learned from it. One day God said to me clear as day. You must read the bible to feed you spirit it is your weapon against the enemy. I thought about it and realized every time I fell it was when I was not feeding my spirit with the word or in prayer. Sheila continued what had evolved into a heartfelt lecture that she was bestowing upon her cousin. "Dwayne, trust God. Laugh at the devil. Know that you are a new creature in Christ Jesus. Old things have passed away and all things have become new. You are going to have a testimony. God is going to use your very life to save souls. If you stick with God, your life will never be the same; it will be so much better. I'm telling you all of this because I truly care about and love you."

Sheila hugged him and gave him a kiss, and he said, "Cousin, I can feel the love of God in you; and it is real. Oh, and from now on, my name is Dwayne. No more of that 'GTM' stuff. Sheila, it feels like I can now see things so much more clearly. Thanks Sheila for taking time to tell me these things. Because I did not know most of this what you are telling me. Basically I have to fight for my life. I can now see that my life before was just foolishness."

At this Sheila started crying and praising God.

Dwayne continued, "My heart just feels as light as a feather. Something inside me is different. I can feel it."

"With a big smile on her face, what you're feeling is the new you in Christ. Doesn't it feel good?" Sheila asked.

"Yes it does!"

"Dwayne, I don't mean to shove this all down your throat but, I am just so happy and excited. When you get home, read Psalm 118: 16-29; and after you see the doctor, read it again. When you get your test results read it yet again. Read the whole chapter of Psalm 118.

"Cousin, when those days come when you feel lonely because you don't have your old friends, just talk to God and tell him what you feel, 'Lord, I thank you for loving me. I thank you for delivering and healing me.'

"You must find and attend a Bible-believing and Bible-teaching church, and become an active member. You have to read God's Word, and know what it says for yourself. I have some information I think will be useful and helpful for you, which I'll get and bring to you."

"I would love that, Sheila. Thanks."

Sheila gives him a big hug again.

"Just always remember that the Bible is your weapon against the enemy. I know that all of this doesn't sound easy right now, so whenever you feel like you need to talk, please call me anytime, day or night. If you fall, get up fast and keep running the race. Your life will never be the same. Your face even looks different now; that's the doing of the Holy Ghost.

"I know I keep saying these things over and over again, but I'm doing it because it is very important. People and your old friends are going to ask you Dwayne, 'What must I do to be saved?'

You have to get away from your old friends. That may be the hardest thing for you because it was for me, especially if they are *not* living their lives for God. They are going to try to get to that old man that you used to be. But when they try, just say to them, 'God has been too good to me for me to go back into that world where the devil was trying his best to kill me.' Then tell them how God has delivered you, when they see you they are going to know that something is different about you. You won't look sick any more and that is when the opportunity will come for you to tell them how God had delivered you," Sheila said, quoting the following scripture:

2 *Corinthians* 5:17 *Therefore if anyone is in Christ, he is a new creation; old things have passed away; Behold all things have become new.*

"Dwayne, you are a new creature in Christ," Sheila smiled as she finished her talk with Dwayne. She was so happy because she could see that God would be using her cousin to save lives.

The thing that gets me is when I think of when the enemy was trying to kill me. Dwayne I believe if did not have a relationship with God I would probably be dead today. I just thank him for his unfailing love that he has for us. When the enemy comes, just say, 'I am redeemed from

72

the curse of the law.' Mother Banks and Kenny, meanwhile, were giving glory to God by dancing in the Spirit, with no music! Somebody got a timbering, and then everybody started to get their praise on, having a good time in the Lord.

Presently, Sheila noticed that more of Tanya's neighbors were peeking over the fence from their back yards. Two of the neighbors, an older couple, had their hands stretched out and were praying.

CHAPTER FOURTEEN
PLEASE PRAY FOR MY FAMILY

At Tanya's invitation, to some more neighbors. As soon as they entered the back yard, One neighbor asked for pray for her family. Sheila called Mother Banks over, and Tanya neighbor related how her husband had been let go from his job when his employer closed down. She also revealed that now her husband would stay out until all hours of the night, something he had never done before while working.

She indicated that his change of behavior was due to his having lost his job, and he was having a very hard time dealing with it. He had always been a great provider, she said, and he was worried about how he was going to pay the bills. She said that their credit cards were maxed out; and that they would have to take their kids out of the private school they had been attending, and send them to public school.

"Our lives have completely changed. Everybody is acting funny around us, and we're hiding our car from the repo man. I'm at my wit's end, and I don't know what we're going to do. We've never lived like this before."

With a deep sigh, and with difficulty, she also admitted that she was beginning to harbor thoughts of suicide.

Finishing her story, she asked for prayer again, and stated that she wanted to accept the Lord as her personal savior.

Concerned over the woman's thoughts of suicide, Mother Banks said, "Honey, every time you have thoughts of suicide, they are coming directly from the enemy — the devil. It is his Job to steal, to kill, and to Destroy. That's what the Bible says, and you had better believe it because it is true. But I'd like to tell you something now that will help you. It's a short story called 'Dead Man's Bones.'"

With that, Mother Banks begins to tell the story.

CHAPTER FIFTEEN
SUICIDE STORY
("DEAD MAN'S BONES")

"There was this lady who was very rich," began Mother Banks. "She had fancy cars, homes, everything she thought she wanted. She gave her family everything. Whenever someone needed something, they came to her and she gave it to them. And then, one day, she made a really bad investment and suddenly, just like that, she lost everything.

"She was devastated. 'There's nothing I can do! I'm going to disappoint everybody, all of my friends, because I won't be able to give them anything now! I'm going to have to walk away from all of this.' Then, she found out that she had to vacate her home in seven days; and she had nowhere else to go because she was too embarrassed to ask anyone if she could stay with them.

"As the days passed, everything slipped through her fingers. All of her cars, her nice furniture, everything, was repossessed, gone. She ended up with one car, some clothes, a few pieces of jewelry, and that was it.

"She was so devastated over the adverse turn of events that thoughts of killing herself began intruding into her mind. As the thoughts strengthened, she resolved that she was going to kill herself.

"And then, she happened to look in an otherwise empty desk drawer, and found an airline ticket to Africa she had purchased a couple of months ago. With all the misfortune that had suddenly befallen her, she had completely forgotten about her planned trip to Africa.

"Turning the ticket over in her hand, she said, 'I'm going to take this trip. Then I'll I will do it. Might as well have a little fun before the end.'

"As she was about to unhook her answering machine, she realized that nobody to whom she had told what has happened to her called her back to offer good wishes or help.

"Leaving the house to run an errand, she happened to drive past her cousin's house, and couldn't help but notice that a big party was going on at their place. People filled the porch and the front yard, and they were all happy, laughing, and having a good time. *Why wasn't I invited?* She wondered, hurt at being left out, and forgotten.

"The next day, trying to find a little solace, she stopped at the house of some people she thought were her friends. When she knocked on their door, and they answered, they acted like they were hesitant to let her inside.

78

Trying to put on a cheerful front, she said, 'What's up y'all?' However, they said hardly nothing. They just sat back down and resumed the game of cards they had been playing with a number of her family members. It was obvious to her that, like her cousin, they were having a get-together: Playing cards, eating, and having a good time.

"She was puzzled that they barely spoke to her, as most of them were among the people to whom she had given things — the very people she had helped. She couldn't believe it. They were acting like she wasn't even there. Before, when they had come to her house, in anticipation of her generosity, they had always hugged and kissed her, and spoke warmly to her. On the weekends, she had hosted the same kind of card parties for fun at her house, and everyone had talked to her. In the good times, she had been the center of much favorable attention.

"Sighing, she thought, *I guess the fact that I've lost everything means nothing to them. I'm no longer of any use to them. Now they're just going on with their lives, and they couldn't care less what happens to me.*

"Leaving the card party shortly thereafter, she returned home. Sitting alone in the house, which was now empty, she continued thinking about how her family and so-called friends were acting towards her. She thought about all the times during which they had come to her house, had fun, ate good food, and swam in her pool — all at her expense. She remembered how the kids had loved coming over to swim in the pool and play games in the game room; and how the adults had loved her bowling alley. Looking around her now empty home, she thought wistfully, *We sure had some great times in this house. But now they all act like none of it ever happened. As if everything I did for them means nothing. They act like they couldn't care less if I live or die. They act as though I'm dead already.*

"Then she started to think about how she was going to survive until she ended her life. *Where am I going to live? How am I going to eat? How am I going to pay my bills?* Just everything was flooding into her head.

"The next day, she went and hocked her remaining jewelry; and, with the money was able to rent a small apartment. Soon came the sad day on which she had to vacate her house, and move to the apartment.

"Arriving in Africa several days later, she was devastated as soon as she saw the appalling conditions under which the people there were living. It seemed as if everybody was homeless.

"However, by far the most disturbing sights to her were *dead bodies* lying in the street, with people walking around and past them as if they weren't even there, like it was nothing. *How can they be so callous as to allow someone's body to just lay abandoned like this in the street? Doesn't anyone care enough to give these poor souls a proper burial? They were* <u>*human beings*</u>*! Does anyone even cry for these poor souls? So,she stoped a lady and asked her why are the bodies in the street like this. She informed her since the earth quake. A lot of people have died and lost their love ones and there is no one to give them a proper burial. Dealing with her own life situation she forgot about the earth quake that happened there. She thought about it and remembered that is why she delayed her trip.*

"When she returned home from the trip, she thought about her life. In particular, she thought about how similar were the way her friends and family were treating her to the way the people in Africa ignored the corpses in the streets. *I might as well be one of those corpses in the street*, she thought. *Nobody cares whether I live or die.* And then, bitterly, she thought, *Once I kill myself, will anyone cry over me or even come to my funeral? Or will they all go to another card party?* She then realized rather she lived or died people are going to go on with their lives.

"In time, however, she managed to find a job in which she earned enough money to pay her rent. She also enjoyed her work, so much so that it took her mind off of the things she had lost. Eventually, all of the money and riches she had possessed in the past came to mean nothing to her now.

"And with that realization came an even more important one: *Why should I kill myself? Why should I end my life just because I can no longer please a bunch of ungrateful people? They don't care that I lost everything. They probably didn't care about me before. They only cared when I had something to give them. And they wouldn't have cared if I had gone ahead and taken my own life. They only care when I have something to give them. So to blazes with them all! I will NOT kill myself!*

"Sparked by her newfound realizations, she began to value both herself and her life. She decided to *live* her life. She decided to learn to *love* herself. She decided to nevermore try to buy peoples' love.

"In time, she wrote a book — an eloquent and compassionate book on suicide and how to prevent it — titled *Dead Man's Bones*. The publisher to whom she submitted it was so impressed with her work, realizing it would be a top seller, that they purchased the book for *one million dollars.*

"However, she didn't tell her family — not about her having written the book, nor about the huge amount of money she had been paid for it.

"On her next visit to family members, she dressed plainly and simply, appearing common and ordinary. Noticing that her relatives were looking at her like she was trash, and acting as though she wished she wasn't there, she asked, 'Why y'all acting so funny?'

"In response, a male family member sneered, 'How does it feel to be off that high horse?'

"'What high horse? Have I ever acted like I was on a high horse? Have I ever treated any of you as though I was better than you? I loved helping my family, and my friends. I always walked in love.'

"Another person, a lady, remarked, 'No, you weren't on a high horse. But the fact remained that you had all that good and expensive stuff, and we had nothing.'

"'Well, whenever any of you came to me for something, I always gave it to you, didn't I?'

"'Yeah,' said a second woman. 'But you got me a car that was *five years old*! I wanted a Mercedes Benz! After all, you had one! You had all kinds of cars!'

"'Is that how all of you feel?' she asked.

"In reply, one of her nieces spoke up — and the whole tone of the conversation changed abruptly. 'Auntie, I'm not ungrateful. I want to thank you for everything you've done for me. I'm just sorry, so sorry, that I didn't say this to you before, when I should have. Please forgive me. If I can help you with anything, I certainly will; please let me know.'

"Looking sheepish, a couple more relatives chimed in. 'You really were nice to us. We should have appreciated your generosity a lot more.'

"Then her niece and her sister stood up and hugged her. Philosophically, her sister said, 'You'll be all right. After all, what you had was just material stuff anyway. When you leave this earth, you can't take none of it with you.'

"Said another family member, 'But I know you must miss living like that.'

"Shortly thereafter, she moved to another state. A month later, she was interviewed about her book on CNN about her book, because there was a high suicide rate in the city to which she had moved.

"Over time, her book touched many people's lives. In fact, it became so influential that the suicide rate in her city dropped dramatically.

"Although she never told her family about the million dollars she had been paid, nor about the substantial royalties she had earned from its sales, during an appearance on *The Larry King Show* Mr. King let the cat out of the bag. 'I understand your publisher paid you one million dollars for your book.' Holding up the book, he continued, 'The title is *Dead Man's Bones*, folks.'

"As Larry King spoke, the woman thought, with a big smile on her face, *I wonder if my family is watching?* And then she thought, *When you live for God, when one door closes He opens another one.'*

"And that's the story of *Dead Man's Bones*," said Mother Banks to the Tanya's neighbor.

"Where did you hear that incredible story?" asked the woman.

"Oh, I didn't hear it anywhere," smiled Mother Banks, a twinkle in her eye. "I'm the author of *Dead Man's Bones*."

CHAPTER SIXTEEN
LIFE IS HOW YOU TAKE IT

Placing a comforting hand on the woman's shoulder, Mother Banks said, "Baby, you don't live your life trying to live up to other people's expectations. If she had killed herself, people would have just kept on living their lives. She would have missed out on her blessings. Maybe she became blessed because she wasn't a selfish person, but a giving person. Don't live your life based on other people; you live your life trusting God. Know that trouble don't last forever. Weeping may endure for the night, but joy cometh in the morning."

Tears streaming down her face, Tanya's neighbor said, "You're right. I can't live my life according to what other people think about me or because of material things."

Motioning the other ministers present at the barbecue to gather together, Mother Banks led them in prayer for the woman and her family.

When the prayer was finished, Tanya served dessert — her homemade cheese cake that everybody loved.

Kenny walked over to Sheila and hugged her, saying, "I have never in my life seen anything like what's happened here today. God was in the back yard of a barbeque, baby. I wish My Mom and Dad could have been here to see it for themselves; they would have had a good time. Honey, when you first started speaking, the Lord just led me to pray in the Spirit. It felt like the Holy Ghost had just moved in."

Walking up to them, Mother Banks pointed her finger and said, "You see, Sheila, what kind of God we serve? We put God in a box too much. If you invite Him in, He will show up wherever you are." Then she shouted, "Hey! Glory to God! Thank you Jesus! This was the best, and the first, church barbeque I've ever been to — and God showed up right here in this very back yard! And I had a ball."

"Yes, he certainly did, Mother Banks!" said Sheila.

"Oh, baby!" gushed Mother Banks. "I am so excited for you and what God has in store for you and this wonderful young man. Kenny and I talked for only a minute, and I love him already. He's a sweetheart. Any time y'all need me, just call me." Shaking her head, Mother Banks continued, "Sheila, I saw two corrected here today."

At this, Sheila went bent over, in awe of God over how Mother Banks had seen what she had seen in the flash.

After the barbecue was over and the back yard was empty, Tanya, her husband Jeff, Sheila, and Kenny sat down at the kitchen table and conversed. Jeff remarked, "I never would have thought it would have turned out like this. The Lord showed up at our barbeque. Man, this was the best barbeque we've ever had! This was the first time we had our whole family come together and pray like this. This makes me want to have family barbeques all the time."

Before Sheila and Kenney left, Sheila gave Tanya and Jeff big hugs and said, "Thank you, I love you guys so much."

In the car on the way home, Kenny was very quiet, which Sheila couldn't help but notice. Finally she said, "Baby, what's the matter?"

"Baby, I have never in my life been as proud of someone as I'm proud of you. Girl, you are the bomb! My chest is sticking out so much it hurts. Baby, the Glory Cloud was all over you. Why didn't you tell me you were a woman with such a bold spirit? I am sitting there like, 'Look at her, she is on fire,' and, baby, you were serious."

Sheila said, "Honey, I never did anything like this before. I just did what I was led to do by God."

Kenny replied, "I was standing there and saying, 'This is my wife-to-be praying up a storm right now.' I told God that He is so mighty and powerful. I was giving him glory. I said, 'She is my other half that you gave just for me, Lord, and she loves you so much. Lord, this is the very

woman I have believed you would send to me, and you did.'
Baby, I jus wanted to run up and give you a kiss and tell
everybody how I had prayed for you, and how God had
given you to me. Baby, I felt like a grand prize winner."

Smiling Sheila said, "That is so sweet!"

"All I am saying," Kenny continued, "is that the way
I feel we need to go somewhere and get married. Or you
need to get away from me. Sheila looked at Kenny and said
"Honey your alright ?:

"No! I am just so full, I need to go home and pray. "
Kenny replied.

The two just busted out laughing. I still feel God's
glory right now; Sheila said. "God is so good honey, and I
am so proud to have you be a part of me."

"Baby, I was thinking the same thing; and you know
what else? I believe that, in time, God is going to give us a
ministry when He releases us for it."

"Honey, I could believe it. I didn't know that you
were such a fervently praying woman as you are. I knew you
loved God, of course, but I didn't know you were bold like
that. Yes I believe he will give you a ministry"

"Honey," said Sheila, "I was not like this before. Not
before today. God is doing something in my life, and I'm

going to go with it. Just know that it's for His glory, not mine, baby. I just move when He says move."

"Baby, you are the bomb!" said Kenny.

As they reached Sheila's place, Kenny grabbed Sheila softly by the face and said I love you so much and I am very proud of you for being the bold women of God that you are. He kissed her on her forehead and Kenny got out to opened the car door for her, Sheila said, "Baby, just take a deep breathe and relax, we need to go to our respective corners and cool off for a while." At this, they both burst out laughing.

Stepping onto her front porch, Sheila and Kenny started kissing passionately. Finally Sheila said, "Baby, you better stop playing, kissing on me like this. You know I'm a righteous woman of God. Call me when you make it home."

"Let me walk you inside," he said.

"Kenny, that's not a good idea because you're not in the Spirit right now; you leaning in your flesh."

They laughed again, and Kenny said, "Honey, listen. I love you. I really and truly do. But I love God first. I will never do anything that will take us outside of His Will."

On that note, he opened her door so she could go in and he gave her a peck on the cheek, said, "Good night, honey," walk away and climbed into his car, and drove away.

CHAPTER SEVENTEEN
BUT I WANTED TO BE YOUR WIFE!

As he drove away, Kenny watched in his rearview mirror as Sheila went into her house. He was giving God so much glory that all he could do was cry in joy, his tears streaming down his face.

As he arrived home, he saw a woman on the sidewalk approaching him. As she walked up to him, he recognized her as Marcella, one of the sisters from the church singles meetings.

"Kenny, what happened?" Marcella began. "We used to talk and hang sometimes, but you don't call me no more."

"Well, Marcella; there's a reason for that. I've found someone, and we're going to get married."

"What? Are you serious?"

"Yes. I am so in love with this woman, I can't describe it in words."

"Kenny, I thought that God intended for you to be *my* husband! I wanted to be your wife!"

With that, she opened up her trench coat, revealing that she only had on some very sexy underwear.

"You know what?" said Kenny. "The anointing is on me so strong that I can see your heart. Come here!"

Grabbing her face, he looked her squarely in the eye and exclaimed, "Demon! Take your hands off Marcella at once! She is in the righteousness of God, and she shall have a husband who will love her and cherish her — and he will be a man of God! In the name of Jesus, I demand that you flee from her immediately! She is a loved woman of God, and God loves her! In the name of Jesus — *flee!*"

Gazing wide-eyed at Kenny, Marcella said, her voice trembling, "Oh my God! I feel it in my heart! God is going to send my husband! A weight has just been lifted off my body! Thank you, Jesus! And thank you, Kenny! I am so sorry. I know that you are a righteous man of God."

"That's all right. I forgive you," said Kenny. Then, with a smile, he added, "Just make sure that you invite me to your wedding!"

"You can count on it," Marcella replied gratefully.

CHAPTER EIGHTEEN
THE BATTLE TO RESIST TEMPTATION

Walking to his apartment, Kenny found his cousin standing by the door waiting for him. "Hey, man, what's up?" said Kenny. "What you doing here?"

"I'm having some problems, man. I need to talk to you."

"Come on in, man," invited Kenny as he opened the door.

Taking a deep breath, his cousin said, "Man, I just had to talk to somebody. Ken Man, I know you're a man of God, and because of that I know you will always give me the best advice. You see, there's this lady who works with me. She is really attractive. She's doing everything she can to tempt me to be with her. She's coming on real strong. No sooner than my girl and I decide to get married. What should I do?"

Kenny replied, "Listen, man, it's just the enemy — the devil — trying to throw temptation in your face. The devil likes to get a man flustered, especially when he's a man of God or married, or both. He sees what's happening with you and this lady as a chance to make you fall. So, you have to take time to think real hard about what's happening.

"Most important, you have to know that the devil is after you for one major reason: He hates marriages, When you find the women you want to be with for the rest of your life, the devil tries to ruin the relationship before it can blossom into a marriage. People don't realize what happens when they get married. So many people have said they were in a relationship for years, but once they got married they ended up getting a divorce a year later. This is often because they've been living together out of wedlock for years, which is not the Will of God. So the devil doesn't have to press them too hard because they are already living in sin. But the moment they get married he throws everything he can at them. Not knowing what is really going on, they fall prey to the enemy, who ruins their marriages.

"As a result, people nowadays are afraid to get married. They are afraid of divorce; and because of that they avoid marriage and live in sin, and fall right into the devil's trap. It's a vicious circle. The devil is saying, "Yeah, I've got you right where I want you — in sin.

"Once you're married, that's when the devil really comes after you. He wants to manipulate you into breaking your marriage covenant with God.

"Marriage is for a man and a women who love one another unconditionally. Not because he has money, or because she has a body that's out of this world. No! Marriage is more than that, much more. It must be founded on a firm foundation of love, not lust. Love is the key ingredient to a successful marriage. If a marriage doesn't include love, it will never survive.

"That is why you must fight against temptation, against lust. It takes a lot of hard work to keep a marriage together. So now, let me ask you this: How much do you love your girl?"

"Kenny, I love her a lot."

"Well, then, man, every time temptation comes your way, just think of how much you love your girl."

With that, Kenny recited the following scripture:

James 4:7 Submit yourselves therefore to God. Resist the Devil and he will flee from you.

Continuing, Kenny said, "It's like you're in a boxing ring. You have to constantly duck blows from your opponent, your enemy. Keep your guard up, duck and move, and use the Word of God as your punches against him. When temptation comes your way, that's how you fight it. This goes for the sisters, too, including the lady where you work. Just know, and never forget, that the devil wants your marriage or your relationship to fail. "Yeah, she might call you gay or a punk when you resist her advances. But that's

OK, because you'd rather know you are in a faithful marriage than to be bound by the devil and filled with shame lies and guilt. So when those put-down words come your way from her, or if she tries enticing you with flattering words, don't respond the way she wants you to. Say something about your bride-to-be, how much you love your intended. Say how deeply you're in love with your girl, and how committed you are to the relationship and your upcoming marriage. That's your first move. Your second move is to immediately get away from this lady and her temptation."

"Man!" replied Kenny's cousin. "What you're saying makes a whole lot of sense. In fact, I think the devil's even been planting thoughts in my head that my girl's been cheating on me. But every time I look at her, and I realize that she'd never do that."

"Man, most women aren't tempted by other men. When most women are truly in love, they don't have affairs. But if they think you're cheating on them, you can be sure they'll confront you about it, in one way or another. And so," Kenny continued, "You have to pray yourself out of this situation. I know it's hard to resist temptation sometimes. But is giving in to it worth messing up your relationship? Are a few minutes of satisfying your flesh worth losing the girl you love so much? Just know this about cheating: It's well worth avoiding, because that way you won't be bringing lies into your marriage. This is particularly important when your woman is a woman of God, because if you're cheating, God is going to reveal that to her. After all, God sees everything that you're doing. You can never hide from him. Even if a woman isn't a woman of God, even if she isn't saved, she'll still be able to sense that something isn't right if her man is cheating.

"And so, man," concluded Kenny, "long story short: *Don't do it!*"

Taking a deep breath, Kenny's cousin said, "Man, I'm going to tell this woman that I'm happy in my relationship. I'm going to tell her that I'm about to get married, and to please respect that, and respect me. That's it. Kenny, I've got a great girl and I love her so much. Thanks for the talk. I feel like a huge weight's been lifted up off of me."

"Man, let me pray for you." Kenny did so. Afterwards, his cousin left in gratitude.

Alone in his apartment, Kenny sat on his sofa and thought about Sheila, and how good that God had been to him. He believed beyond any doubt that Sheila was the woman God has chosen for him. She was twice of everything that Kenny had hoped his woman would be.

Closing his eyes, he started to pray. "Lord, this woman is funny, smart, and so very beautiful inside and out. Lord, thank you so much. She is special beyond my ability to express in words. She is perfect for me. Sometimes, I feel like I can't do enough to show her how much I truly love her. If I could, I would marry her today. Lord, please help me to calm down and to accept that we will be married in Your Time, according to Your Will. Lord. But if it is Your Will, Lord, please let us be married soon. Lord, search my heart, and if there is anything in it that is not aligned with Your Will regarding Sheila and me, please remove it from me."

Finished with his prayer, Kenny sat and gave God glory.

CHAPTER NINETEEN
SAVED SISTER GETS A MAN

Arriving home from work one day, Sheila noticed that there was a message on her house phone. It was from Saved Sister, excitedly telling Sheila to call her back. Sheila did so, and Saved Sister immediately told her, "Girl, I met someone at the singles meeting! A great guy!"

"Oh my God!" gasped Sheila. "Are you serious?"

"Oh yeah!"

"Who is he?"

"He's a deacon at the church. His name is Deacon Jones. Sheila, he told me some stories about some of the women he's met at the singles meetings. How they tried to entice him into drinking and fornicating. And then he told me he was so happy the night he came and met me! He also said he had come to that meeting intending it to be his last one."

Bursting into laughter, Saved Sister continued, "He even told me that he thinks one of the ladies spiked his coffee with something. He said she invited him to her house for coffee. He somehow fell asleep there, and woke up to find that his shirt was off and she was kissing all over him! He said that he jumped up and shouted, 'Woman! What are you doing?' then grabbed his shirt and got out of there fast. He said that when he got to his car, he started laughing at himself, thinking what a shame it was for a man his age to be running away from a woman. Then he got real serious, and said that this is the sort of temptation where a lot of men fail because they don't run away from such women, but give in to them. He said these women are messed up from being in so many bad relationships.

"When we first met, he gave me the third degree, questioning me about my life in the Lord. I was like, 'Hold on a second! I should be giving *you* the third degree!'

"'Look,' he said. 'I love God with all my heart, and I am a saved, righteous man.' Sheila, it was so funny — me and my saved self being interrogated by a man about being saved. It just tickled the stew out of me, and he was so serious. These women have put him through the flux.

"Sheila, on our first date we went out for coffee and we talked for hours. We stayed until the coffee shop closed. The next day we went to lunch. I haven't had this much fun in so long! Oh my God!

"But, Sheila, I still can't believe this man was actually questioning me about my life in the Lord. He told me he didn't have any time for games. He said that if I wasn't a woman of God, he didn't want to get involved with me, and waste his time or mine. He also said that God is coming back soon, and he wants to be right for God because he loves Him so much. Girl, when that man said that, my heart felt like it just dropped to the floor. Girl! Girl! Girl! He's a handsome man, too! He doesn't look his age.

"It was so cute; all I could do was laugh. I was sitting there thinking, *Lord, so many women are looking for a man of God; and here is a man of God who is terrified of women!*

"After he gave me the third degree, I asked him why he had approached me in the first place. He said he had noticed me, saw that I was active in the church, and liked the way I carried myself.

"This weekend we're going fishing. Sheila, I have a feeling this man is going to ask me to marry him. I wasn't expecting this. I was going to the meetings just to help out with serving the food and stuff. I wasn't even thinking about finding a man. I always said that if I would ever be with someone, he would have to find me because I wasn't looking. And that's exactly how God intended for it to be.

"Well, girl, I just had to talk to you and tell you about my honey bun. I would have told you before, but I wanted to make sure that he wasn't a jokester or a player."

"Praise God, Saved Sister!" exclaimed Sheila. "You deserve to have a good man. Like you said, you weren't even looking — and look what God sent you."

"Sheila, I'm so excited! I'm having such a good time with him. We have so much fun together, and really enjoy each other's company. If he asks me to marry him, I'm going to say yes. But enough about me. How are you and Kenny doing?"

"We're doing just great. Saved Sister I am so happy for you. I am sitting here floored with your testimony. But I've never been so happy in my life!"

"Praise God! Well, I got to run. Tell Kenny that I said 'Hi' and that I'm praying for both you guys. Call me when you're ready for some help with your wedding. Love you and Brother Kenny. Bye now."

Hanging up the phone, over joy by Saved Sister's wonderful news, Sheila made herself a cup of coffee. Then, sitting down in her favorite easy chair, she opened her Bible to do a little reading.

CHAPTER TWENTY
BROTHER FRED CALLS SHEILA

As she sat leafing through her Bible, and absorbing its wisdom, she thought about all of the wonderful things that God was doing in her and her friends' lives. *It's just like He is pouring out His Love all over the place*, she thought.

Later that night, Brother Fred called. "Sister, I just want to say that you had the Glory Cloud all over you at that barbeque, and oh, how you were praying, sister! Do you hear me? I am so happy for both you and Kenny. Who knows what would have happened if you and I had gotten together. Maybe it would have worked out; maybe it wouldn't have. But, oh my god! Kenny is so blessed! But you know what, Sis? God knows all things. When we step back and give Him full control, He just blows our minds every single time with his awesomeness. I see God blessing you guys with a ministry."

"Brother Fred, I've been thinking exactly the same thing, and you've just given me the confirmation that it's really going to happen."

"Well, praise God! And please accept my thanks and gratitude for bringing Nollie to the singles meetings and helping me to meet her. Sheila, I think she is the one. But please pray for us; and please tell Kenny to call me so that we can make plans for the four of us to hang out."

"We'll also be calling you about the plans for our wedding."

"Great!"

"Brother Fred, I feel like God just took my heart and read the blueprint. He has blessed me with my every desire, and I am so happy."

"Praise God, Sis! I am so happy for you guys. Well, just call me and Nollie and let us know the wedding date and what we can do to help."

"I sure will, and I'll have Kenny give you a call."

"Oh, I almost forgot!" said Brother Fred. "The church of a friend of mine is having an anniversary service. You think you and Kenny could make it over?"

"I'll ask him, but I'm sure we'll be able to go. When he calls you, you can give him all the information."

"Thanks, Sis. Bye for now."

"Good bye and be blessed, Brother Fred."

As she hung up the phone, Sheila had no idea that the actual purpose of Brother Fred's phone call was to set up a complete surprise that Kenny had in store for her. Knowing that Sheila loved surprises, Kenny had planned a good one.

CHAPTER TWENTY-ONE
GOD'S SUPERNATURAL POWER

Kenny and Sheila arrived at the church for the anniversary service for Brother Fred's friend. As soon as they walked through the door, a strange feeling came over Sheila. Taking their seats, Sheila was startled by the familiar thunderclap sound— only this time it was louder than ever. Sheila thought, *What was that, Lord?* Turning, she looked at Kenny, and it was obvious that he hadn't heard it. Wondering what would happen next, Sheila braced herself. She was certain that God was about to do, or show her, something really big.

As the anniversary service commenced and proceeded, Sheila got into the service somewhat, but was still bracing herself. Finally, she let go and whispered, "Lord, just use me according to Your Will."

The instant Sheila said these words, the Lord took over. Looking around at all the people in the church, Sheila could see their spirits and see into their lives. Some of the peoples' spirits were perplexed, some uneasy, and others happy; it was just amazing. When she looked at Kenny, she could see that he was so happy and complete, and at peace having overcome a previous heartache.

She could also see, as clear as day, the crowns of the men.

Noticing the intensity in her eyes, Kenny asked, "Honey, are you all right?"

"Yes, I'm fine," she smiled, Remembering what mother Banks had told her.

As she continued observing the people, Sheila could see things that people were dealing with in lives almost as though God were telling her, their life stories. But she had no idea why. And then the following words came to her mind:

When you pray and ask God to use you as a vessel, open your minds to no limits, and just go with the flow. For, He is God. Just act as though He has you by the hand. You cannot be in fear, or He won't be able to use you.

Taking this admonition to heart, Sheila suddenly realized that God was showing her the spirits and lives of these men and women for a specific purpose according to His Will. This caused her to relax and think, *OK, Lord, I can deal with this. I know you are showing me these things for a reason.*

Presently, the service turned to high praise of the Lord, with people shouting and getting into the Holy Ghost.

It was as though everybody was going through something or another, and decided that they had to get their praise on. Sheila could tell that the people were serious, and had pressing real-life issues.

The service then went into worship, and everyone began singing the song, "Here I am to worship." As the singing reverberated throughout the church, the Glory Cloud entered the building.

Pastor Jones, the church's pastor, asked for every available minister to come up to the front of the church. "God is in this place," he stated, "and He is about to do something. So move quickly." Sheila felt as though she should join them, but she remained where she was, thinking, *He's not talking to me. I'm not a minister, after all.*

But then, with crystal clarity, the Lord said to her, **Sheila, go up to the front,** and she obeyed immediately. Walking towards the front of the church to join the ministers, Sheila could feel her heart pounding — but not out of fear, but out of her excitement in knowing that God was about to do something significant. As soon as she reached the front of the church, she heard the thunderclap, and thought to herself, *OK, Lord, whatever is about to happen, use me. I am ready.*

With that, she began to pray in the Spirit. Looking up, she saw that many people were kneeling face-down on the floor, including the pastor. Impelled to do so, Sheila picked up the microphone and began speaking, allowing her words to be led by the Holy Ghost.

"The Holy Ghost is here right now, and is here to deliver you. Don't stop praying. If know you should be up here. You should get to this alter. I am not calling you up here not to talk about or embarrass you, but to *love* you and to help you be delivered.

"Every last person in this church has to make the decision to come up to the altar — if not right now, then sometime soon. But you must come to it at some point.

"Every last one of us was born into iniquity. All of us have sinned. If you say that you haven't sinned, then you lie and the truth is not within you. You are not the first to sin, and certainly won't be the last to do so. But know that God loves you more than you could possibly ever realize. Indeed, He died on the Cross just for you and your sins.

"The Lord is here, the time is now. The Lord says that someone here has been diagnosed with a terminal disease. To that person God says, "***Repent and turn away from your wicked ways and you shall live and declare the works of the Lord.***"

"Someone in this church is fornicating with someone else who is also here. God says,

"Repent and turn away from your wicked ways."

"Someone here is cheating on their spouse. God says,

"Repent and turn away from your wicked ways." You know exactly who you are and what He is speaking of.

"Someone here is stealing from this church. God says,

"Repent and turn away from your wicked ways, take up your cross, and follow Me."

"Some in this church are living the bisexual lifestyle. God says,

"Repent and turn away from your wicked ways."

"Ladies and gentleman, the Holy Ghost is here to deliver you. God loves you so much. If you want to be delivered and set from your burdens, come forward to this altar."

By now the altar was filled with people, and Sheila continued. "The Lord is about to take this church and make it grow like never before. It will be so packed; there will be standing room only. God is setting you free today. He is calling upon you to become apostles for Him. You are going to be intimately involved in this movement of God. This is

111

not a game. The devil is not playing, so we must all be all about God's business.

"You will not allow people to come to you and sway you with the old stuff like temptation. Those things have passed away, but the Word of God abides forever. You have been redeemed by the blood of Jesus Christ. Today is the day. If you love God with all your heart, mind, soul, and strength, you will stand at this altar and nevermore be influenced or tempted by people and what they think or say about you. People, after all, don't have a Heaven or a hell to put you in.

"I want everyone in here to close their eyes and picture Jesus on the Cross. In your minds, I want you to place at His feet. Every problem, every hurt, every pain, every disease — everything inside of you that you don't want — place it at His feet. Every situation and burden — lay it at his feet. He loves you. Give it all to Him right now.

"People, this is not me speaking these words. It is the Holy Ghost speaking every word through me. There is a John here; God says that He knows your heart and to give it all to him. There is a Denise here; lay your burdens at His feet. Pastor Jones — lay your burdens at His feet. A woman here has just learned she's pregnant and HIV-Positive. Don't kill that baby. He bore our sicknesses and diseases at the

Cross, and so the price has been paid. Everyone, repeat after me: 'Father, forgive me for I have sinned. I repent and turn my life over to you, Lord. Lord, I confess with my mouth and believe with my heart that God raised Jesus from the dead. And now I am saved."

With that, Sheila started laying hands on people, and as she did they fell like dominoes. Turning to Pastor Jones, Sheila said, "Pastor Jones, I realize that you don't know me from Adam, and I didn't intend to take over the service like this. But God told me to do so, and I must do what God tells me to do. I thank you for not intervening in this movement of God. I don't know these people; I've never met them before. I was just invited by a friend for the anniversary service."

In a reassuring tone, Pastor Jones said, "Sister, I knew you were genuine when you gave voice to issues and problems my congregation had told me of in confidence, but had told no one else because the matters were too personal.

"You are right that I don't know you; but I do know that you are acting according to God's Will. I thank God for your being obedient and doing what God has told you to do. Whoever you are, and wherever you come from, one thing is certain: God is in you, and there is 101-percent pure Holy Ghost in you."

"Pastor Jones, my name is *Sister Sheila*, and this gentleman standing next to me is my fiancé, Kenny. We were invited here tonight by our mutual friend, Brother Fred, for his friend's anniversary service. In truth, I believe that the Lord invited us all here tonight. Praise God!"

Everyone exclaimed "Amen!" as Pastor Jones gave Sheila and Kenny warm hugs.

After the service was over, Sheila and Kenny stepped outside, and Kenny went to get the car. As Sheila stood waiting for him, a lady came up to her. "So, you're Kenny's fiancée," said the lady.

"Yes I am. And may I ask to whom I have the pleasure of speaking?""Sheila, replied."

"I'm Marcella. Kenny and I used to hang out before you guys met. But now I understand. He got just what he believed God would bless him with — a woman on fire for God. He told me the other night that you guys were getting married. Honey, you got a one-in-a-million fine man who loves God wholeheartedly. I wish y'all the best; but I really don't have to, 'cause God is moving in y'all's life already. Just imagine what's to come! Please, woman of God, give me a hug."

The two women embraced, and then Marcella started walking away. As she did, she said to Sheila, "You stay blessed."

Kenny pulled up in the car. As they drove towards Sheila's place, she remained very quiet, and he noticed a sober expression on her face. "What's wrong, baby? You OK?"

At this, Sheila began crying like a two-year-old. "Baby, what is it?" he asked in genuine concern.

"Oh, Kenny! I just can't express how happy God has made me! I've never prayed so fervently for people or spoken so boldly as I did at the barbeque especially tonight. And I certainly never prayed for people at the altar before. Baby, it was as though God had full control of my mouth and body.

"I think about all those nights when I prayed and asked God to send me a man who loved Him and who would love me, too. I think about the times I prayed and said, 'Lord, I want to be a vessel for Your Glory.' And now it's all come true. He is using me for His Glory, and it feels so good, like a high that you don't want to come down from. I feel like saying, 'Lord, let's do it again! Praise God!

"First He gives me you; and then He uses me for His Glory. Praise God!"

Kenny took and tenderly held her hand. "Baby, I know exactly how you're feeling right now," he said. "That's just how I've been feeling ever since our first coffee date. It's the feeling that you love God so much, you wish there was a way you could just kiss Him and give Him the biggest hug ever. But, honey, He already knows how much we love and adore Him. After all, He knows our hearts."

Leaning over, Kenny kissed Sheila softly and said, "Honey, let's go grab something to eat. I'm starving from all that excitement!"

"Me, too," Sheila smiled.

CHAPTER TWENTY-TWO
THE SURPRISE(S)

Kenny and Sheila stopped at a very nice restaurant for dinner. Taking in the place, she said, "Honey, this place is really nice. Don't you have to make reservations first?"

Smiling, with a twinkle in his eye, Kenny said, "Don't worry, everything's been taken care of."

As they sat down to eat, Sheila noticed two older couples sitting across from them. They appeared to be in their sixties. Suddenly, the thunderclap sounded, there was a flash, and Sheila could see the crowns of the two men, both crowns leaning to the left. *Oh, Lord, no!* thought Sheila, realizing that the positions of the crowns indicated their worldly lifestyle. She barely noticed when Kenny excused himself from the table and went to the restroom.

Alone at the table, Sheila continued observing the crowns. Presently, one of the men looked up and noticed Sheila's gaze. He smiled at her and she returned his smile. Knowing that it was God's Will, Sheila stood and walked up to their table.

With no preliminaries, she said, "Hi. My name is Sister Sheila. I'm sorry for interrupting your dinner. But I have learned to be obedient to God whenever He tells me to do something. Do you belong to a church?"

They said no.

Handing them her business card, she said, "Whenever you feel like you want to go to church, please feel free to call me. I will even pick you up and drive you if necessary. Sorry again for my intrusion. Enjoy the rest of your dinner."

Returning to her table, Sheila hoped that they would accept her invitation.

"Honey, you OK?" asked Kenny as he returned and sat down.

"Yeah, honey, just a little tired."

As soon as they were finished with their meal and the plates were cleared from the table, Kenny solemnly took Sheila by the hand. "Honey, you know how much I love you, right?"

"Yes, of course I do!"

"Well, I have some wonderful news. My employer just gave me another promotion, along with a company car. The thing is, I can't drive two cars. Now I know that your car is working all right. But it's more than ten years old, and I think it's time you had an upgrade, don't you think?"

"Baby, what are you saying?"

Smiling broadly, Kenny said, "What I'm saying is that I want to give you my car. It's much newer and in much better operating condition."

"Oh, thank you, baby!" gushed Sheila.

"Now, just make sure you promise to take care of it, OK?"

With a warm laugh, Sheila said, "Of course I will, honey. I promise."

Then he said, "Will you please shut your eyes?"

"Say again?" Sheila raised an eyebrow quizzically.

"Please, shut your eyes," he repeated, with a mischievous grin. "Humor me."

"All right, baby," said Sheila, shutting her eyes but having not the slightest idea what was going on.

"That's good. Now, don't open them until I say so."

"What's up with you?" Sheila asked, feeling silly closing her eyes in the middle of an expensive restaurant.

A moment later he said, "OK, Sheila, open your eyes!"

The instant she did, she saw Kenny in front of her, with one knee on the floor. In his hand he held a small box containing an absolutely beautiful, glittering diamond ring.

"Sheila, will you be my wife? Will you marry me?"

"*Yes!*" she screamed in delight, and everyone in the restaurant broke into loud, enthusiastic clapping as Sheila and Kenny kissed warmly to seal the deal.

When the noise died down, Kenny said, "Come on, honey. It's been a big day. By the way, you can drive if you want," he smiled. "After all, it's your car!"

Stepping out of the restaurant, Sheila noticed a car in front of the restaurant with a big bow on top of it.

"Wow, somebody is about to be happy!" she said, admiring the beautiful shiny car.

Kenny replied, "Oh, one thing, honey. Please forgive me, but I'm afraid I told a little fib in the restaurant. I'm not giving you my car. I'm giving you *this one!*" he handed her a Lexus keychain.

Utterly stunned, Sheila started screaming and crying. "Oh my God! For me? I don't know how much my heart can take! Thank you! Thank you! Oh, Kenny! I love you so much!" With that, she hugged him tightly and began kissing him like crazy.

"Girl! You better stop kissing on me like that! After all, I'm a respectable man of God!"

They both laughed heartily, and climbed into the Lexus — Sheila in the driver's seat, and Kenny in the front passenger seat. As Sheila pulled the car out of the parking lot, she asked in amazement, "How did you pull all of this off?"

"Brother Fred helped me. He drove it here for me. We've been planning and working on this surprise for weeks! The anniversary service at the church was actually a pretext to allow me to bring you to this restaurant tonight without arousing your suspicions. But neither I nor Brother Fred had any idea what was going to happen at the service. I must say that both of us are more in awe of God than ever. After what happened at the church, I hope my proposal and my little present tonight haven't been too much for you, honey."

"No, honey, not at all. I love your sweet, little heart. I feel as though God is pouring His love on me. Baby, you can't beat God and His giving. He is so awesome and mighty. He loves us so much. I just thank God for you. You are the best next thing to Him. I'm filled with joy. All of my dreams have come true. Praise God! For He is true to His word." That said, Sheila recited two scriptures that both she and Kenny well knew:

Matthew 6:33 Seek you first the kingdom of God its righteousness and all things shall be added unto you.

Mark 11:24 *Therefore I say unto you what things so ever ye desire when ye pray, believe that ye receive them, and ye shall have them.*

"He is so true to His Word," continued Sheila. I give Him all the glory and honor and praise. Oh, baby, he gave *you* to me! I feel like he made you just for me."

"Honey," smiled Kenny, "You're going to have to put me out of this car in a minute. You're starting something!"

"I am so happy that you were so persistent."

"Girl, I told you before: From the moment I first saw you, I claimed you as my wife. So you weren't about to get away from me. It was a wrap for all them other brothers. It was like I took a branding iron and stamped my name on your forehead!" They both shared a good laugh at this.

Arriving at Kenny's apartment building, Sheila parked at the curb. Before Kenny could exit the car, Sheila cupped his face in both of her hands and said, "I thank God for you. You wonderful man of God. I can hardly wait to become your wife."

They exchanged a passionate kiss, then Kenny replied, "Baby, me too."

Then, her face breaking into a mischievous grin, Sheila asked, "Would you like me to walk you in?"

"No!" he laughed. "Because, you are all up in your flesh right now! I might even have to put some blessing oil on you!"

Kissing her tenderly, Kenny climbed out of the car, saying, "Good night, baby. I love you."

"I love you, too," Sheila smiled warmly.

CHAPTER TWENTY-THREE
"I WANT TO KEEP MY HUSBAND!"

One day, Sheila was in the cafeteria at her workplace, having lunch, when a young woman who worked with her came up and sat down beside her.

"Sister Sheila," began the young woman, "I saw you at that anniversary service the other night, and I never realized that you were a woman of God like that! I already knew you were in the Lord; but, my God, I never imagined how much!" Sighing deeply, the woman continued. "I really have to talk with you about something very important. I hope it's all right."

"Why, certainly," smiled Sheila. "What's troubling you?"

"I need help so that I don't revert back to my old ways. Because if I do, I'll ruin my marriage. I'm having some really serious problems, and I need God to help me. I cheated on my husband in the past, and I'm afraid that temptation will make me do it again."

"Have you prayed and talked to the Lord about this yet?"

"Oh, yes. In fact, after that night seeing you at the anniversary service, my life changed. I'm really not the same person that I used to be. Following the service, I went straight home to my husband and confessed. I told him, 'Honey, I have not been a good and faithful wife to you. I've cheated on you. But I promise that from this day forward you will be the happiest married man alive. Can you possibly ever forgive me?' To my joy, Sister Sheila, he told me that, yes, he forgave me; and I just cried in happiness.

"Since that night, our house has seemed like a whole new home," continued the woman. "Sheila, God has truly been so good to me! I am sold out for him. In fact want to get into a Bible-teaching church, so that I can learn the Word of God."

That said, the woman's smile faded to a worried frown. "But, Sheila, lately my old feelings of temptation have started creeping back into my mind again; and they're getting stronger all the time. I'm fighting to resist them and stay faithful to my husband. But I'm afraid I'm going to succumb to them and stray again. And if I do, my marriage will be destroyed. What can I do? Oh, Sheila! I want to keep my husband!"

"Girl, you have to build a strong and firm relationship with the Lord. And to start building that relationship, you must know, acknowledge, and accept that He knows your heart. He knows your thoughts before you

126

think them, He knows your words before you speak them. So keep it real with him. Tell Him the truth. Tell Him your fears. Tell Him your feelings. And tell Him what you want and need. During the anniversary service, did you lay everything at the altar and repent?"

"Yes," said the woman.

"Praise God for that! So, whenever the enemy — the devil — tries to cause temptation to rise up within and overwhelm you, you have to rebuke him. You have to say, 'I am redeemed from the Curse of the Law!' This means that the price has already been paid for all of your sins. Jesus Christ died on the Cross to make it so. And at the altar the other night, you repented and gave the burden of your sins to God. That burden no longer belongs to you. Praise God!

"Girl, people have to learn to live life for themselves and not care about what people say or think about them. This is very important. People not of God will try their best to get you back to doing the same old, bad things you used to do, like cheating on your husband. This is one of the main ways that the enemy tries to steal you back. His job is to kill, to steal, and destroy says the Bible. He wants to wreck your marriage, and ultimately to destroy you. What this means is, you are going to have to walk away from all of your old friends. All of them. Find and join that Bible-teaching church you mentioned. I can recommend some fine ones. Get into that church and be active in it. Go to the Bible study meetings and pray. Praise God! Now I must ask you, is your husband saved?"

"Yes, he is."

"Well, praise God! how would y'all like to come and hang with me and my fiancée, and our friends? We'd love to help both you and your husband strengthen your relationships with the Lord."

"Oh, Sheila! I would love that — and I know my husband would, too!"

"So, girl: What are you going to say now when the enemy tries to bring back those old thoughts of temptation?"

"I will say, 'I have repented, for God has forgiven me!' I will say, 'Get under my feet, devil!'"

"Amen!" Sheila said. "The Bible tells us that the devil is the accuser; he wants you to have burdens and stresses. But, again, you have to know that those burdens and stresses are now done and over with. You have been forgiven. Give God glory for His Grace and Mercy. When there is a problem in your life, look in the glossary of the Bible. There you will find listed, for whatever problem you have, scriptures dealing with exactly that problem. Turn to those scriptures, read them, and see what the Bible says about that problem. In that way, you will learn for yourself what God has say about your particular situation, and how to resolve it. Girl, I want you to know that I will be praying for you."

"Oh, Sheila! From the bottom of my heart, thank you. If I could, I'd love to show my gratitude by inviting you and your fiancé to come over and have dinner with my husband and me one night."

"Why, thank you. We'd love to do that. But, girl, I really haven't done anything. The Lord did, through me. So you must give the glory to God, not to me."

After work, while Sheila was in the grocery store, her cell phone rang. It was Nollie.

"Girl, you have to come right over here!" said Nollie anxiously.

"What's wrong? Are you all right?"

"Yes, everything's fine. You just have to come over."

"OK. I'll be there in a few minutes."

As soon as Sheila arrived at Nollie's place, Nollie asked, "Sheila, is it true that Kenny got you a Lexus?"

"Yes, darling, it's true. That's it in the driveway. In fact," Sheila smiled, handing her the keys, "go ahead and take it for a ride."

"For real, girl?" Nollie stared incredulously at the Lexus keychain she was now holding in her hand.

"Sure! Go ahead, girl!"

As excited as a little girl on Christmas morning, Nollie climbed into the Lexus, pulled out of the driveway, and drove off down the street. Returning a few minutes later, Nollie stepped out of the Lexis with a look of pure happiness.

"Girl, that man must love you so much!" squealed Nollie. "I didn't know about the Lexis. But when Kenny and Brother Fred went to pick out your engagement ring, they had me come along to give them advice. And let me tell you, girl, Kenny didn't care about prices. He just said to me, 'Which ring you think Sheila would love? Not like, but *love*?' So, I looked them all over — and when I saw that special ring, something in my head just said, 'That one.' Well, not 'something'; it was the Holy Ghost. Sheila, this man loves you so much. I've never seen love like this in a man in all my whole life. You are so blessed to have a man love you like that."

Hugging Nollie, Sheila said, "Girl, you got the exact same love with Brother Fred!"

CHAPTER TWENTY-FOUR
GET DOWN, FLESH

Nollie said, "You're right, girl! This is crazy. Both of us got good men of God. Some days I can't believe it. But now you know I've just turned my life over to the Lord, and I go to Him about things I need His help with. Brother Fred's spirit is so sweet. Some days I feel like,

" *God, is this for real? Could this man one day really be my husband?* "

"But, Sheila, this man turns me on so much, I have to wrestle with my flesh sometimes because I just want to give myself to him! One day I ran in the bathroom and locked the door because I wanted to wrestle him to the floor at that very moment! Sheila, I was in the bathroom saying, 'Help me, Jesus, please!' I know Brother Fred's a man of God. How do I stop myself from wanting him so bad like this?"

Sheila said, "Wait Nollie, you ran in the bathroom? I don't mean to laugh. I know this is serious Listen, girl! You're only human. But you have to cast that temptation, down. When your flesh comes up like that, you have to talk to it. You have to leave, or put him out until you cool down.

Do whatever you have to do to stop yourself from going there, from giving in to temptation. Tell your flesh to get down. Say, 'I am redeemed from the Curse of the Law.'"

So saying, Sheila recited the following scripture:

Galatians 3:3 *Christ has redeemed us from the curse of the law. Having becoming a curse for us (for it is written cursed is every man that hanged on the tree.)*

Sheila continued, "Nollie, having given your life to God, you have the right to the promises of God. Just start praying, because you don't want to give in to temptation; you could lose Brother Fred if you do. After all, just like Kenny, he wants a woman of God, a woman he can be in accord with. I know it's hard sometimes, girl, because I get the same feelings, too, and so does Kenny. You don't know how many times we've been parked in front of my place, and I've had to jump out of his car and run inside, pray, and take a cold shower. But I've done that because, first and foremost, I don't want to displease Kenny, myself, or, most of all, God. So just hang in there; everything will be all right."

CHAPTER TWENTY-FIVE
"WHAT'S WRONG, HONEY?"

Leaving Nollie's house, Sheila called Kenny and told him that she was on her way home to fix dinner for him. He said he would be right over.

The moment he stepped into her apartment, Sheila could tell immediately that something wasn't right.

"What's wrong, honey?" she asked.

"Nothing, baby," he said only half-convincingly.

To brighten the atmosphere, Sheila said, "Kenny, guess what? You know when I was praying and the Lord said somebody was pregnant. Well, guess who it is?"

"Who?"

"My sister Tanya!" Sheila grinned. "She and her husband Jeff had given up, but she finally got pregnant. But you know what, Kenny? When I said that someone was pregnant, I never dreamed it was her, because they had tried everything to conceive. They even said they weren't going to try to have kids anymore. They accepted it, and thought maybe it was not in God's will for them to have children. But, baby, they are so happy now!"

"Honey, that's wonderful news. I'm so glad for them," responded Kenny, but with a lack of enthusiasm that Sheila couldn't help but notice.

Sheila said, "Are you hungry? Dinner's almost ready."

"Yes," he answered, again with little enthusiasm.

"OK, baby," Sheila looked directly at Kenny. "What's up? The two of us are one. I know it's not official yet, but as far as I'm concerned we are one. You and I have no secrets to hide from each other, unless God says so. Obviously you're upset about something. Now, if your problem is not sealed by God, I'd feel much better if we could talk about it. If you don't feel like it right now, I can respect that. But, honey, I'm your other half, remember? I feel in my heart that I can confide completely in you. And you have to know that you can confide completely in me."

Kenny looked at her and said, "Honey, I hear you. When I'm ready to talk about it I will, OK?"

"OK. Fair enough. But I must ask you this: Do you still love me, Kenny?"

"Well of course I do! With all of my heart, Sheila," he said in all sincerity.

"OK," smiled Sheila. "Now, let's sit down and have dinner. Then I'll give you one of my *good kisses*!"

With that, Kenny pulled Sheila to him, hugged her tightly, and laid a kiss on her that was so passionate her knees buckled.

"Girl, you OK?" he chuckled.

"Oh, yeah! You won that round!"

Later, as Sheila and Kenny relaxed on the sofa after her scrumptious dinner, the phone rang.

"Nollie," said sheila, "I need to ask you about something important."

"Sure, what is it?"

"How would you feel if Brother Fred and I eloped?"

"What?!? Are you serious, girl?" gasped Sheila. "Why would you do that?"

"Well, don't the Bible say it is better to marry than to burn?"

"Of course it does, Nollie. But have you talked to Brother Fred about this? What does he think?"

"I just broached the subject on the phone with him a few minutes ago. I don't know what he thinks about it yet. He's on his way over here right now so we can talk about it."

Sheila took a deep breath. "Nollie, you two have to get some marriage counseling."

"Why? Why do you need counseling if you love someone? You love them and that is it."

"No, Nollie, there's a lot more to marriage than that. Marriage is a covenant between you, your husband, and God. That means it's a serious matter. You don't marry someone because you lust for them. You have to know what the Word of God says about marriage. Because when the trials of married life come up, and they always do, you have to know how to deal with them. You can't just say, 'This isn't working; I don't want to be married any more.' For instance, if Brother Fred lost his job, what would you do?"

"I guess I'd have to get a job, or even two, to tide us over until things got better."

"What if he said, 'Nollie, we're going to have to be on a tight budget, so don't go shopping until I find work'?"

"Well, I guess we'd just have to be on that budget."

"And what if because of his job, or a future job, he has to go on the road for months, and you hardly get to see him?"

"Well, I'd just go with him if I could."

"What would you do if you ever felt he wasn't paying attention to you?"

"I'd come right out and tell him I was feeling ignored. Then I'd do something to add some spark to our romance."

"Girl, you got an answer for everything. But please don't think I'm asking all these questions as a put-down, because I'm not. I'm asking them because you need to know that there's more to marriage than people realize. A successful marriage takes a lot of hard work. Nowadays, people give up and get divorced over the least little thing. You're my dear friend, and I don't want that to happen to you and Brother Fred. So now, the most important question of all: Do you think Brother Fred loves you?"

"Oh, yeah. Sheila, I have never felt so loved in my entire life. Adam gave me material things. But that doesn't compare with having someone who really loves you for *you*. Like when a person looks at you and just smiles. Or like all the little things that he does just because he's eager to put a smile on your face. Brother Fred calls me just to ask how my day is going and if there's anything he can do to make it better. We go for walks by the water. He takes me and my daughter to the park. And he's so nice to her, as well. He always tries to put a smile on her little face. She's crazy about him. Sometimes, she asks about him before she asks about her daddy."

"Nollie, I'll come over tomorrow after work, and we can talk about more about this. For now, though, I just want to tell you that I don't think you should elope. That would just be putting too much pressure on him into getting married in a hurry. It would be much better to take your time, and have a proper wedding, girl."

"OK, Sheila. Thanks for all your advice. See you tomorrow. Bye."

"What's up?" asked Kenny.

"Oh, Nollie's tripping. She wants Brother Fred to elope with her."

"That's not good, Sheila," Kenny shook his head. "It's just not right. Brother Fred's a man of God, and Nollie shouldn't be trying to coerce him into eloping. Actually, I found out about this just before I arrived here tonight. I'd just finished talking to Brother Fred before pulling up, and he told me what Nollie had said."

"Is that why you've been upset since you got here?"

"Yeah. I most definitely don't think they should elope. That would be jumping into marriage too soon."

"I agree. In fact, I told Nollie they should get some marriage counseling."

"I hope that Brother Fred doesn't go for her idea. After all, I would hope he knows better than to do something rash like that."

Sheila said, "Well, honey, we just have to pray for them." She paused, then continued. "On the other hand,
138

could it be that they'd elope and everything would be just fine? Is it really our place to sit here and pass judgment on them? After all, we both know about people who meet one day, get married the very next day, and live happily together for the rest of their lives. So, you really never know."

"Sheila, what do you think would happen to us if *we* got married, or even eloped, without any marriage counseling?"

Sheila pondered Kenny's question for a moment, then answered, "Actually, honey, I believe in my heart that we would be just fine. Because I know that this right here, what we have together, was divinely ordered by God. But I would not get married until I had prayed about it and spoken with my pastor."

Kenny said, "Well, I want you to speak with your pastor, honey."

"Why, Kenny? Do you mean…you want to elope, too?"

Gazing lovingly at Sheila, he said, "Yes. Why not? Like you, I believe our relationship has been divinely ordered by God. And I think everything would work out fine for us. So…shall we do it?"

"Kenny, I would love nothing more than to become your wife right now, at this very moment. But I've given this a lot of thought; and I want us to get married the right way, in a proper wedding."

Looking at Sheila with newfound respect, Kenny smiled and said, "OK, honey, if you want to wait, then I'm fine with waiting, too. I want you to have exactly the kind of wedding that you want."

"Honey, our wedding doesn't have to be fancy or expensive. All I need is my wedding dress and *you*! That's all I'm asking for. For our honeymoon, it would be so nice if we could go somewhere really romantic for a week, if we can. But I know you have the new job, so if you can't take time off, we can go on our honeymoon later."

"Sheila, I want you to have that honeymoon, and I want it, too." With that, Kenny pulled out his cell phone and checked his calendar. "Why don't we get married on September the Seventeenth? I could that next week off, and that would be ideal for our honeymoon."

"That would be perfect!" Sheila happily said. "That'll give us enough time to plan a proper wedding, consult with the pastor, and go for the marriage counseling."

Kenny took a deep breath. "Baby, do you really want to go through with this? I certainly do. Ok here's the deal take my black card get the dress that you want. Honey don't go crazy using this card. Sheila said" what is my limit."
140

He said get what makes you happy.

Baby don't get a crazy wedding planner. My cousin had one and she was ridiculous.

Sheila said." Because I love you I will be reasonable honey". That is why I love you girl.

"Baby two months and you are all mine, Kenny!" said.

Sheila, eyes were filled with tears of joy. Then, kissing him tenderly, she said, "Baby, watch a movie with me."

They did; and before it was half over, Sheila fell asleep...

She awoke with a start when the phone began ringing. The morning sunlight was coming in through the windows. Rubbing the sleep from her eyes, Sheila looked around. Kenny was gone. *Oh my word!* she thought. *I slept all night and half the morning!*

Picking up the phone, she said, "Hello?"

"Hello, Sheila! It's Nollie!"

Sheila couldn't help but notice the elation in Nollie's voice.

"What's up, girl?" asked Sheila.

"Girl, my toes are curled up and I can't uncurl them! Brother Fred and I are in Las Vegas! He and I...we..."

"Nollie! No! You *didn't*!"

"Yes! We eloped late last night! Drove straight to Vegas! Went into one of those 24-hour wedding chapels! And…Sheila…We're *married*!"

Sheila was so stunned at the news that she couldn't speak for a moment.

"We are *sooooo happy*!" said Nollie. "Lord Jesus! That man of mine had me *speaking in tongues*! I'm about to go back in there for another round — with my *husband*! So, I'll call and talk to you tomorrow, OK?"

"Sure. And Nollie? Congratulations! To you both!"

CHAPTER TWENTY-SIX
WHERE'S KENNY?

As she got ready for work, Sheila picked up the phone and dialed Kenny's number. There was no answer. The same thing had happened that night, just before Sheila had gone to bed. *I wonder why he's not answering the phone?* she thought. Figuring that maybe she had just missed him twice, she shrugged it off.

During her lunch hour, Sheila took out her cell phone and dialed Kenny again. Still no answer — and now Sheila began to worry. It wasn't at all like Kenny to not answer the phone if he was home; or to not call her for more than a day.

Her worry mounting through the rest of the day, as soon as Sheila left work she immediately drove to Kenny's apartment building. She knocked on the door, but there was no answer. Explaining the situation to the apartment manager, and her concern that Kenny might be in trouble, the manager unlocked the door and they both entered Kenny's apartment. Everything appeared in order, but there was no sign of Kenny.

Her worry giving way to real fear, Sheila then drove to Tanya's house to see if she knew what might be going on with Kenny.

Arriving at Tanya's house, Sheila found her in the company of the neighbor woman who had been considering suicide the day of the barbecue. Now, however, the woman was going on and on with gratitude about how God had answered her prayers. She said her husband had found a job, based upon favorable recommendations from his previous employer. She told Tanya and Sheila that as soon as her husband had given her the news, he had given his life to God. The woman concluded by saying, "Thank you for letting me come over that day and for you guys praying for me! God is so real!" With that, she gave Sheila and Tanya big hugs and left.

Now alone with Sheila, Tanya asked, "Hey, Sis, you look really worried. What's going on?"

Sheila said, "Sis, I'm really getting worried. I think maybe something's happened to Kenny. I haven't been able to reach him by phone for a couple of days; he hasn't called me; and he's not in his apartment. I don't know what's going on, but I have a bad feeling about this.

"Sheila, don't entertain any negative thoughts. No way has Kenny run out on you. The two of you are made for one another, and that's that. Sometimes men just go through a spell where they have to go off for a bit and be by themselves to sort things out. Sheila, I know that man loves

144

you. After all, what man would buy a woman an expensive car like that Lexus, not to mention such a beautiful and expensive a ring like that, if he didn't think the world of you? Girl, you're good. Something's going on with him, and he has to sort it out. That's all. So just let him have his space, and don't tell no one else about this. And try not to worry too much. You and I are going to walk in faith, and know that everything is going to be all right."

Laying a reassuring hand on Sheila's shoulder, Tanya continued, "Hey, I've got an idea, Sis. Tomorrow let's go to the bridal shop, just you and me. After that, we can go to check out some wedding planners. That'll take your mind off this until Kenny calls. Sheila, I just bet that right now he's somewhere putting himself before God. So, listen — don't doubt him, trust him. Now, let me put on some shoes and grab my purse. What we're going to do right now is go out for some ice cream!"

A short time later, as Sheila and Tanya sat in the ice cream parlor, Tanya had an idea. "Sheila, why don't you try texting Kenny?"

"Why, that's a great idea, Sis! Thanks! I don't know why I didn't think of that." Reaching into her purse, Sheila removed her cell phone, and composed and sent off the following text to Kenny:

Baby, I haven't heard from you in a couple of days, and am really starting to get worried. I hope you're all right. I'm with Tanya right now. She's going to help me pick out my wedding dress. Then we're going to choose a wedding planner and start with the arrangements. If you don't want me to do this, for any reason, you need to say something quick. — Love, Sheila.

Not a minute later, Sheila received the following text in reply:

Everything's fine, baby. Sorry about not calling. Something came up I've had to attend to. Please, get whatever dress you want, and use my credit card. And by all means go ahead with starting the arrangements too. I love you so much! Will call & explain everything soon. — All My Love, Kenny.

Smiling, Tanya said, "See, Sheila? What did I tell you? That man *loves you* and wants to *marry you*! It's all good! So let's go pick out that dress of yours, and get this wedding show on the road!"

Tears of gratitude in her eyes, Sheila said, "Thank you so much, Sis! I love you!"

"I love you, too, silly woman! Even though you worry way too much!"

CHAPTER TWENTY-SEVEN
TEST RESULTS

When Sheila arrived home, she was surprised to find that Kenny had been there; he had left her a box of chocolates, with a bow on top, and had brewed some coffee for her. She immediately dialed his number; but, as before, he didn't answer. Now she was more puzzled than ever.

Suddenly the phone rang. Thinking it was Kenny calling at last, Sheila grabbed the phone and anxiously said, "Hello?"

The caller, however, wasn't Kenny but Adam.

"Hey, Sheila. I went to the doctor to get tested for HIV. And you know what? All the tests came out negative! But I have to be tested again in six months, but I'm perfectly healthy!"

"Praise God, Adam!"

"Did you tell Nollie I was going in for the testing?"

"Adam, I'd never reveal your or anyone else's personal business. When God tells me to be discrete, I am. After all, He knows everything — including if I violate His or someone else's trust by opening my mouth. You know, Adam, I have to laugh when I think about people who do something and think nobody else knows. They seem to forget, or to have never learned, that God, who is in Heaven and who can save us from Hell, knows everything that everyone of us is doing. So, no, Adam I didn't tell Nollie. This matter is strictly between us, and God."

"I thank God for you, Sheila, because unlike so many people, you don't judge me and talk about me, as flawed as I am."

"Adam, we all fall far short before God. None of us is perfect. Indeed, every last person on this earth was born into sin. Only Jesus Christ was perfect. Adam, please promise me that from now on you'll never care about what people say or think about you. Just know that God loves you, and that is all that matters. Whenever you want to talk, you can call me or Kenny. We got you back."

"Thank you so much, Sheila. I'm going to tell Nollie about my testing because keeping it from her is bothering me. So, please pray for us, because I know my having kept this a secret from her is going to be hard for her to deal with. I'm just thankful to God that I won't have to tell her I'm HIV-Positive."

"Good for you, Adam. You know Nollie is like a sister to me, and I love her. So, yes, I will be praying for you guys."

Two hours later, Sheila tried yet again to call Kenny — but still no answer.

After a few days, Sheila still couldn't reach him, nor did he call her. She put up a front that everything was fine; but inside she was extremely upset and confused. *Whatever on earth is going on with Kenny?* She wondered anxiously.

One afternoon, Nollie called and asked, "Sheila, could you please come over soon? I really need to talk to you."

"Sure, I'll be right over," said Sheila, sensing by the tone of Nollie's voice that Adam must have told her about the testing. "Nollie, are you OK? You don't sound so good."

"I'm not, to be honest."

"Baby, I'm on my way."

Pausing before opening her apartment door, Sheila prayed, "Please, God, help me find the right words to say when I talk to Nollie. Amen."

Arriving at Nollie's place, Sheila could instantly see that her friend was a mess. Normally Nollie was a diva when it came to her personal appearance; but her hair was uncombed, she looked unkempt, and her face was etched with worry. Taking her hand, Sheila asked, "What's going on?"

"Sheila, I have to tell you this first. When Brother Fred and I got married, I felt no guilt at all. The only thing that I felt was happiness. I married that man because I love him, and I believe with all of my heart that he loves me and my baby, too. It wasn't just all about being intimate with him.

"Well, Sheila, the day after we got married, I had to go to the car for something. And as soon as I opened the car door, something just came over me. I can't even describe it. The feeling was a peace and joy that I had never felt in my life, and tears just came down my face. I thought, *God, you did this for me?* and then I said, 'Lord, I am so sorry for every time I have disappointed you.' Please, Lord, forgive me.'

"Sheila, the tears were just running down my face, and they felt like they were coming right from my heart to God. Like my tears were saying thank you to God. I said to Him, 'I don't believe I have ever known true love like this, God! I never knew that love could feel so wonderful!' You know, Sheila, true love brings a peace that is indescribable. I never felt like that with Adam — I guess because with him being married, I never had him to myself, and I always felt guilty about having his baby with him being married.

"So, I never felt there was anything like true love between me and Adam. But then God blessed me with Brother Fred, a saved Christian man, who helped me turn my life around and live for God. Sheila, I am so happy you took me to that singles meeting. I guess maybe all those years you've been praying for me are finally paying off. I'm so happy and grateful that you stuck by me and didn't walk away from our friendship after you got saved."

With that Nollie and Sheila hugged, and Sheila said, "Girl, I'd never have walked away from your or your friendship! But now, girl, tell me what's wrong."

CHAPTER TWENTY-EIGHT
DOWN LOW CONFESSION

Nollie sighed deeply, then began. "Sheila, I don't quite know how to tell you this, so brace yourself. Adam came here yesterday, and apologized for the way he had been treating me. He said that ever since he gave his life to God, God has been revealing some things to him, and He has changed his heart. He said he is not the man he used to be. He said, 'I have to confess something to you, Nollie. But before I do, just know that from the bottom of my heart I am truly sorry. Also, Nollie, I know about the preacher and I know that he's been really nice to you. I just want to say that I'm so sorry for having put you through all of this; you deserve so much better. I will always love you and our baby. Please, don't let what I'm about to tell you mess up what you have with that preacher man. He's a good guy, and I feel perfectly comfortable with him being around our baby. Please hear and believe what I'm telling you. I have repented and asked God to forgive me; and I ask you now to forgive me as well, Nollie. I have been on the down low. I didn't think it was because there was any penetration, but I allowed this person to do stuff to me. A man! Not a woman! A *man*! You hear what I'm saying? He gave me all kinds of money, and that is how I was able to do things for both you and my wife at the same time'."

Nollie paused for a moment to collect her thoughts, then continued. "Sheila, Adam then broke down and cried like a baby. He said, 'Only by the Grace of God was I spared contracting HIV!' He was crying so hard that he made me cry. That's the first time I ever saw him cry; before, he always acted like some kind of hard, tough guy. But I know that he was sincere and truly sorry. That's because I know that God is changing me, too. Yes, I was shocked by what he told me, that he'd been doing another guy, risking HIV, and risking transmitting HIV to me. And if I'd still been the old Nollie, I would have just flat out got my gun and shot him then and there with no remorse. But instead, I felt no hurt, no fear; my heart just forgave him without me thinking twice. I told him I was very proud of him to be man enough to come to me and tell me because he didn't have to. I know that it was nothing but God on him.

"Sheila, I feel like my life is becoming a fairy tale that God is controlling. I feel like true inner peace is at hand for me at last. But here's what I'm worried sick about. Although I've forgiven Adam, how am I going to tell Brother Fred what Adam told me? Should I even tell him? What would Brother Fred think if he found out that in the
156

past I was having relations with a bisexual man who could easily have contracted HIV and spread it to me? What would Brother Fred think of me? Would he still love me? What in the world should I do? Here I marry this wonderful man of God — and now I find *this* out!" Nollie's voice trailed off, and she burst into tears.

Putting a comforting hand on Nollie's shoulder, Sheila said, "All you have to do is to pray about this matter to God, and He will reveal to you what you need to do. Just pray and trust in God. Don't give in to fear. After all, fear is from the devil. And we know that when God has authority over our lives, the devil loses every time. Right? So that's it, Nollie. Be happy and thank God that He sent you this wonderful man — this *understanding* and *forgiving* man of God — who makes your toes curl up in knots! Praise God!"

"Oh, Sheila! Thank you! I love you so much!"

Arriving home a short time later, Sheila ran quickly inside, hoping and praying that Kenny was there waiting for her. He wasn't. But in the middle of her kitchen table stood a large and incredibly beautiful arrangement of flowers that he had left. She also found, resting on her coffee table, an enveloped addressed to her, in his handwriting.

Carefully opening the envelope, Sheila removed a letter, handwritten and signed by Kenny, and started to read it.

As she read his words, Sheila's eyes and mouth opened wide in shock. Finishing the letter she said, her voice shaky, "Oh my God…!"

TO BE CONTINUED

FINAL THOUGHT

My book is for men and women who just want to find a good person who is able to love. But, for real, there are good men and good women out there who, perhaps because of bad relationship experiences, are afraid to take the risk of seeking out the good and loving persons they long for. They want to love the way love was meant to be, but have lost all hope of being able to do so.

Nowadays, moreover, many men and women are simply too selfish to allow themselves to love just one person. Also, there are many women to every one man.

If you live your life the way God intends, and if you pray fervently, however, then He will send to you the right man or the right woman, gift-wrapped, just as you've been praying for. That person will be tailor-made for you. Praise God! We just have to trust God and do what we need to do.

Every woman, it seems, is looking for the perfect man — especially if he's a real man, one who steps up and pays the bills; fixes the car; takes the family to church on Sunday; provides for the household; loves his wife, and her only; loves his children; and makes time for his family.

Please believe me. There really are men out there like that, trust me. Men who, furthermore, will not stray from their marriages and be tempted by loose women who try to seduce them.

Women, this goes for you, too! There are good men out there who are looking for good wives, too! So, women, you have to have your stuff together. If you don't know how to cook, then get a cookbook or go on the Internet and learn. A good man wants a woman who is independent, smart, and knows her business in the kitchen and in the bedroom (this latter only when you're married, though). Keep the house clean, ladies; and love him, don't nag him. If you don't trust him, walk away because the relationship will never work out. You must be able to trust the person you are with. If you don't, if you can't, such will lead to problems. Either check yourself to make sure you're being a good woman; or, if you realize your man is a good man, learn to trust him. If you still have that vague uneasy feeling of mistrust in your stomach, then he is not the man for you.

The bottom line in all of this is the Word of God, as revealed in *Ephesians 5:21-33:*

Ephesians 5:21 Submitting yourselves one to another in the fear of God.

Ephesians 5:22 Wives, submit yourselves to your own husband as unto the lord.

Ephesians 5:23 *For the husband is the head of the wife, even as Christ is the head of the church: and he is the savior of the body.*

I want you to read all of these scriptures in full. By doing so, you will gain a better understanding of what God's Will is in regards to marriage.

I once heard the story of a lady who was celibate for almost thirty years, had four kids, had long since come to terms over being a single woman, and never strayed from God. But it was God's will that she not remain single. So, wouldn't you know, God put her in a certain good man's path, and they met at a store. Then they crossed paths again. In time, they struck up a friendship. Both were up in age; but eventually, he asked her to marry him. She did. She said he was tailor-made for her.

This very same thing has happened even to people who were not living for God he has no perspective of people. He loves us all.

THE COVENANT BETWEEN MEN AND GOD

The title of my book is *The Crowns of Men.*

Why did I write this book, and why did I give it that title? I did so because God just put the book in my spirit and I just began writing it.

I believe that men are very special to God. Adam was the first human that God created from the dust of the earth. He even chose Noah to build an Ark. Abraham was very special to God also. He used Moses to lead the people out of Egypt. Job was special to God, as. There are many more men in the Bible that are very special to God.

Genesis 2:7 *And the Lord God formed man of the dust of the ground, and breathed into his nostrils the breath of life, and man became a living being.* (Adam)

Genesis 17:7 *I will establish My covenant between Me and you and your descendants after you in their generations, for an everlasting covenant, to be God to you and your descendant after you.* (Abraham)

Genesis 17:10 *This is my Covenant which you shall keep, between me and you and your descendants after you every male shall be circumcised.*

Genesis 6:9 *These are the generations of Noah: Noah was a just man perfect in his generations, and Noah walked with God.*

Genesis 6:13 *And God said unto Noah, The end of all flesh is come before me; for the earth is filled with violence through them: and behold, I will destroy them with the earth.*

Genesis 6:18 *But with thee I will establish my covenant with you; and you shall go into the Ark.-you, your sons, your wife and your sons wives with you.*

Crowns are for Honor and Glory

Psalms 21:3 *For thou presences him with the blessings of goodness: thou wearest a crown of pure gold on his head.*

1 Corithians 9:25 *And everyone who competes for the prize is temperate in all things. Now they do it to obtain a perishable Crown. But we for an imperishable Crown.*

James 1:12 *Blessed is the man that endured temptation: for when he is tried. He shall receive his crown of life. Which the Lord hath promised to them that love him.*

LEADERSHIP

God created men to be leaders of people. God leads the men, and the men lead the people. Then men can lead their families, their communities, their countries, etc. It is men to whom everyone looks for security. The presidents of the United States have all, thus far, been men. The majority of pastors are men.

Let's face it: On this earth there are men, women, and children. When something untoward happens, everyone looks to the men for the solution. When there is a robbery or an assault, everyone turns to the man of the house to do something. Children look up to their fathers as mentors. Most troubled teens want and need a male mentor. The heart's desire of every woman is to find a good man who will love her. Just about every woman's dream is to have a good man whom she can love him and from whom receive the same.

But there are some men with less than honorable agendas and motives; and there are such women, as well. Trying to find true love among such individuals is futile.

Many women seek the love of a man because they did not have fathers to raise and love them, and so they crave that fatherly love that they never had. Similarly, many men seek love because they failed to receive the love they needed from their parents.

Women are always finding ways to express their love. And it is their hope that the men in their lives realize the existence of that love — and return that love.